Lily

Book 1

The Seer Series

Lily © 2017 RM Walker

Cover Art © Bound2BeSpecials

This is a work of fiction and while some of the places named are real, all events and characters are fictitious and in no way represent real people.

Edited by Jennifer Leigh Jones and Rebecca Stewart of Bookends Editing. www.bookendsediting.com

Contents

Another Move 4
Twins 9
Touch 18
Fae 24
Different 32
French 50
Aye! 65
Friendship 77
Moving Again 85
Holding Hands 98
Rain Check 112
Crowder Manor 122
Jonas 142
Sharing 154
Crocodiles 161
The Seer 175
Drew 195
Acknowledgments 200

Another Move

Moving was easy when you knew how. And Lily knew how better than most.

She couldn't remember a time when they weren't moving. She'd learnt to not hoard things. She didn't collect things she couldn't pack up and take with her easily, like friends. She was friendly with people, she just didn't make any close friendships that she would miss. It was easier that way.

They moved once a year, usually at the end of the academic year in July. There had been a couple of times when they'd moved midterm, but that was rare. Her mother tended to wait until she had finished an academic year before moving on again. The education syllabus stayed mostly the same despite where they were. The only changes were the four walls and the faces around her. She was a quick learner, achieving grade As or Bs; so, despite the disruption of moving each summer, her work didn't suffer.

Her mother, Lynda, had an itchy foot of sorts. But it wasn't wanderlust that moved her, it was the constant urge to paint what she saw around her. Her mother was an artist, and an excellent one. She specialised in sea and landscapes, and her work always sold well. The revenue from her paintings, and a small inheritance from her parents, gave them the ability to move to pastures greener on a regular basis.

And move on to pastures green they had just done again. Her mother was contacted by someone she'd sold a painting to previously. They asked her to do a series of paintings of their home and gardens through the four seasons. So, for the next year they would be living in a small, two bedroomed cottage in a Cornish village that looked as if time had forgotten it.

They'd lived in a lot of places over the years. Mostly in large towns. This was the first time she'd lived in a village, and especially one as small as Trenance. Woods edged the village on three sides, with the sea just beyond the south woods. The positive side, according to her mother, was a bus service that ran to the local town eight miles away. The negative side was that it only ran four times a day. There was a pub and a few shops; a small grocery store that also doubled as a post office, a butcher that did a side-line in fruit and veg, and a bakery. That was it.

Theirs was a typical small cottage, set in between two identical cottages. Lily's room was at the back, and from her window she could see flowerbeds either side of a lawn that led down to the woods beyond. It was a definite improvement on their last home; her window there faced the brick wall of the house beside them.

She sat on the window seat, watching the trees. A light breeze coaxed the branches into a swaying dance. The leaves echoed the sounds of the sea that lay just beyond. But nudging the edge of her senses, there was a wisp of something different. Something beyond her understanding.

"Settling in, honey?"

She looked over her shoulder to see her mother leaning on the doorjamb, her arms crossed over her chest. Lily knew she would be watching her closely for a few days, and she understood that.

"It's an improvement from the last place in Brighton," Lynda murmured, moving across the room to place a hand on Lily's shoulder.

"Yeah, it is." She'd seen so many different views from bedrooms she'd lived in, but she would admit that this was the prettiest view yet.

"I'll take you to college on Wednesday, but according to the Headmaster, there's a bus service that runs to pick up the kids. It leaves from the War Memorial every day at seven, and you catch it again from the college grounds coming home."

"Thanks." Lily nodded her head. She could catch the bus the first time, but it was almost a tradition now. Her mother would take her to school on the first day. Lily thought it was to try to make it up to her for how difficult it was to keep starting new schools every September. She'd never vocalised it though, and her mother never said anything either.

"Have you given any thought to universities yet, Lily?"

"Not yet." Her mother's hands tightened on her shoulders in reassurance.

She would be eighteen at the end of the month, and this was her last year in college. Once she finished college, her life would change dramatically. If she went to university, they would need to stay put for the three years it would take her to get a degree. Lily couldn't remember the last time she'd stayed in one place for more than a year. Leaving somewhere was never as hard as it should have been though. It was the thought of staying in one place for three years that seemed odd to her now.

She wasn't even sure yet whether she even wanted to go into university. Nothing really appealed to her; nothing called to her. She was floating along, adrift, unsure in which direction her life was going to take her. She considered a few careers, but something always held her back. As if she was waiting for something. She just didn't know what that something was.

"There's no rush yet. You can have one of those gap years if you want." The edge in her mother's voice was clear. An edge that was put there by Lily's epilepsy.

"I don't know what I want to do yet," she revealed quietly.

Lily's epilepsy had grown increasingly worse as she got older. When she was young, the seizures weren't too bad, but what started as absence seizures morphed into tonic-clonic seizures. Her mother took her to all sorts of doctors and alternative therapists, but nothing helped. Until one day her mother came home with some tablets that a herbalist gave her. Lily's desperation reached a point where she was willing to try anything. To their relief, they'd worked. Several months could pass without any seizures. When she did get one, it was still so debilitating that she would sleep for twenty-four hours to get over the migraine it left her with. Currently, she was at her best so far; it was six months since her last seizure. She was not allowed to learn to drive a car until two years passed seizure free. She could ride a bicycle, and she did, but it was impractical for long distance journeys. Not being able to drive would put limitations on her future, and she was acutely aware of this.

Lily's father died when her mother was pregnant with her. There were no pictures of him, and Lily knew very little about him. When she had been old enough to start asking questions, her mother's answers had been vague before changing the subject. Lily stopped asking questions, aware that it was a touchy subject for her mother.

"Something will turn up, Lily. It always does." Her mother squeezed her shoulder lovingly. "If you want to choose university, I'll be right there with you, Lily. I can paint wherever you are."

She placed her hand over her mother's, leaning back into her. Her mother meant it, but their track record would suggest that a three year stay somewhere might not work.

"We could find somewhere close to whatever Uni you choose; or you can get those courses that you can do from home. That might even be easier, considering."

"I'll think about it," Lily whispered, feeling her mother kiss the top of her head.

"We have the rest of this year to look forward to first. We aren't going anywhere yet!" Her mother spoke briskly, dropped another kiss on her head and then moved away from her. "I need to ring Mr Crowder; see when I can pop by to start prelim sketches."

She went out, her footsteps echoed going down the cast-iron spiral staircase that descended into the living room.

    Lily looked back towards the forest, running a hand through her dark hair. Her future was so uncertain. Where would she be this time next year? She'd never really worried about it before. Her mother always chose where they were going. But Lily wasn't a child anymore, and she knew there was a time coming where she would have to make her own way. It was more than that, if she was honest. It was as if everything she knew was about to change, that nothing would ever be the same after this year. And that scared her.

Twins

Tuesday morning found Lily standing in her tutor group classroom. Held in a tight grip, she had the map and timetable the office receptionist had given her. Nerves assailed her. Some things never got any easier, no matter how many times she did them.

She kept her eyes on the teacher, her cheeks burning hotly under the curious stares she knew she was getting from the classroom full of students. A short, stout man in blue cord trousers and a thick Aran sweater sat on the front edge of his desk. He looked to be in his early forties, with dark hair that was shot through with grey at the sides.

"I'm Lily Adair. I'm new here, sir."

He gave her a warm smile that reached his brown eyes. "Go ahead and find a seat. We're just starting."

Not making eye contact with anyone, she made her way through the rows of students already sitting; aware that all eyes were still on her. It was a walk she had done numerous times before, but it was never easy. Her cheeks burned as she sank into the seat of the only empty desk in the room. She put her bag on the desk, making sure not to look at anyone.

"Right, now everyone is settled. I hope you've all had a good summer and you're ready for your final year. It's an important year, folks, so start as you mean to go on. Let's get the register over and done with, and then you can all sort yourselves out. Quietly."

Lily took the opportunity to look around for the first time now that everyone had lost interest in her. Like a lot of colleges Lily attended, this one had four houses; Columbus, Raleigh, Cook, and her own, Drake.

"Lily Adair, got you already." She heard him say her name, and then he began calling out other names in the register. She watched as different ones responded to their names, but she knew it would be a while before she remembered who was whom. She had even left some schools at the end of the year still not knowing the names of all her classmates.

"Jake Nethercott."

"Yo!" The lazy sounding voice caught her attention. She looked over and did a double take, two identical boys sat side by side.

"Josh Nethercott."

"Here."

They were two seats over from hers, but it was easy to see they were identical. Straight, tousled, black hair fell into their eyes, touched the tips of their ears, and brushed the collar of their black jackets. They were pale, no signs of a tan, with firm jawlines. They were like two gorgeous peas in a pod. As one, they looked towards her, as if they knew she was watching them. Her cheeks grew even hotter, and she looked away quickly. She waited a beat and then chanced a sideways look back at them, but they were still looking over at her. In sync, they winked at her, identical smirks tilting their lips. Certain she was about to combust, she turned away abruptly, determined not to look back again.

"Okay, everyone, keep the noise down until the bell rings," Mr Peters called out, and taking the register, he disappeared through a door that had Chapter House written on it in gold script.

"Hey, Lily." The girls in front of her, turned to her. "I'm Sarah. Where've you moved from?" The fair headed one spoke first.

"Brighton." Lily gripped her bag tightly in her sweaty palms.

"Cool, we went there for our holidays last year. It's a nice place. I'm Beth, by the way." She flipped her dark hair away from her face.

"Brighton was alright, I liked it there. We've moved into Trenance now; it's very pretty," she told them.

"My aunt lives there. It's okay but too quiet for me," Sarah said, opening up her timetable. "What have you got first?"

"Maths and then English Lit," she said, looking up from her timetable.

"I've got Art and Design, then Drama," Sarah said.

"I've Biology and Physics. What other subjects are you taking?" Beth asked.

"English Language, French, History, and Geography," Lily replied, checking her schedule.

"You'll be back here with old Peters then," Sarah said with a grin. She flicked her long blonde hair over her shoulder. "He's not so bad, but watch he doesn't catch you chatting or he'll throw balled up paper at you."

Lily smiled and looked over to where Mr Peters had emerged from the Chapter House and was in deep discussion with two boys at the front of the classroom.

"That's Wayne and Royston," Sarah said. "They're captains of the chess club. Competition level, and Mr Peters is the lead teacher. We're going up against Burnham College next month and then on to the county finals in the new year, if we get through."

"Do you play?" Lily asked, making Sarah snort with laughter.

"God, no. My brother used to when he was here. He left last year and is now at Exeter Uni."

"What's he studying?" Lily asked.

"Theology and Philosophy. He wants to teach Religious Studies."

The bell rang for the end of registration, and Lily got up along with everyone else.

"Do you know where you're going yet?" Beth asked her. "It's the opposite direction to us or we'd show you."

"Thanks, I'll find it. I have the map they gave me in the office."

"Which was drawn by a drunk two-year-old." Sarah shook her head with a laugh. "You'll never find anything looking at that thing. Wayne said he has Maths first, follow him and you won't get lost."

"Okay, thanks." Lily gave them a relieved smile, and they waved as they joined the rest of the students leaving the room. Lily held back, trying to spot Wayne in the crowd leaving the room.

"Hey, Lily Newbie, where're you headed?" She turned at the sound of her name and saw the twins heading towards her, bags over their shoulders.

"Maths," she replied, and they nodded, almost as if that was what they expected her to say.

"Same as us. We'll make sure you don't get lost, Lily Newbie."

"Thanks."

They smiled at her, and she found herself smiling back. Close up, she could see their eyes were grey. She really couldn't see a difference in them. She'd met identical twins before, but there were subtle differences between them. Differences, that when they stood together, she could tell which was which. But these boys? She couldn't see anything that would help her work out which was which. And it didn't help that they were dressed identically in the college uniform.

"I'm Joshua, he's Jacob. And we'll be late if we just stand here."

She coloured up again and hastily made her way out of the classroom. They directed her left and then fell into step with her, one on either side.

"Where're you from?" Josh asked her, or at least she thought it was Josh.

"Brighton." It wouldn't be the last time she said that during the day.

"Brighton Rock," Jake said with a grin. They led her through a maze of corridors, not saying any more. She didn't know if they were waiting for her to speak or not, but she didn't really have anything to say; first day nerves always stole her tongue. They were good looking, but there was something about them that unnerved her. She put it down to how identical they were.

"Here we are," Josh said, pointing to a door with Mathematics Department printed on it.

"You have a whole department for maths?" She was impressed. Her last college had one room for the entire school and only two classes in each year.

"Well, it likes to think it's a department. O'Connor is department head. He had that put up last year, when he finally managed to commandeer the walk-in storage cupboard from Computer Science. Gives him three rooms, which became the Department," Josh replied. Or was it Jake? He pushed the door open and motioned for her to go first. She thanked him and went through, her eyes taking in the large room that held rows of tiered seating and fixed desks. They were arranged in a semi-circle that faced a giant whiteboard. The front seats and the back ones were already taken, but no one wanted the middle section, and they were all empty. She made her way up the steps and settled herself down, noticing that the twins took desks directly behind her. She looked around. There was a door on either side of the whiteboard. One was marked *Trig and Calc* and the other *Foundation*. Someone had tagged a piece of paper below the *Trig and Calc* sign saying, *O'Conner's Kingdom*.

She turned back to the twins. "Thanks for bringing me here."

"You're welcome, Lily Newbie," one of them said. But again, she had no idea which.

"What've you got next?" the other one asked her.

"English Lit."

"We've Biology next; in the other direction. Have you got that map they give out?"

"Yeah." She turned and drew it out of her bag. One of them reached forward and snagged it from her. He laid it out on his bag and took the pen his twin held out for him.

He snorted as he looked down at it. "You couldn't find an apple in an orchard with this crap. Give us your timetable too," he demanded, and she handed that over without even thinking about it.

The door banged closed, making Lily jump and turn to face the front.

"Right, you horrible lot! Once again we meet, so as you know you can call me Master Jedi, Sir, or Mr O'Connor. I'll answer to any of those. Most of you reprobates I already know, some of you I may not. Newbies to this class, raise your hand, please."

Lily put her hand in the air and wasn't surprised when she was the only one.

"And your name is?" He looked directly at her, shaggy white eyebrows above black rimmed glasses wiggled impressively at her.

"Lily Adair, sir," she answered him.

"You must be new to the whole area as I don't recognise your face at all. Alright, stay there, I'll be with you in two shakes of a lamb's tail. Rest of you carnivorous lot, get your books from the shelf, you know the drill by now. Yes, Mr Watson?"

"Master Jedi, I turned vegetarian over the summer hols. I'm no longer carnivorous."

"Ah, do you eat fish still?"

"Yes, sir."

"Right, Watson, you're a pescetarian, get yourself over to the shelves then!" He clapped his hands, and Lily knew this was a teacher she was going to like. He was tall and thin with wild scraggly hair to go with his eyebrows. And it looked as if he dressed in the dark. She was almost certain his cardigan was inside out.

He took the steps two at a time and gave Lily some papers he had picked up from his desk first. He sat himself on the edge of the empty desk next to her. His cardigan was indeed inside out.

"Don't take this the wrong way, but I don't know you or your abilities from Eve, and I have no desire to read any records which may or may not arrive before you graduate." He smiled at her, his eyebrows doing that dance again. "So, for your benefit, but mostly mine, I want you to sit and go through this test today. If you prefer quiet to the mad ramblings of this crew, you can sit in the Foundation Room as it's empty now."

"I'll be okay here," she said quietly, reaching for her bag. "But thank you, sir."

"No worries. If it gets too manic, just up and pop out there, okay?" He looked up and suddenly jumped to his feet.

"Ah, Nethercotts! Good to see you both back again. Which one are you?"

"Josh, sir." Amusement coloured his voice, as Josh stopped beside her desk. He set a thick textbook down for her, and she realised he'd fetched one for her as well.

"Wonderful! You know the drill, young man. Every class, don't forget!" He held out an orange button badge that Josh took with a quick smile. She watched him put it on the front of his jacket where it could be seen clearly, and she realised it was so Mr O'Connor knew who was who.

Josh sat back down, and Lily turned to him. "Thanks for getting me the book." She grinned at him. "Any chance you can keep the badge on for the rest of the year?"

"Not even one." Josh smirked at her. "Where's the fun in being identical if we can't confuse people?"

She turned back to her test. Mr O'Connor moved off to talk to someone else as she drew out her pencil. She shut out everything around her and concentrated on the paper in front of her.

She was finished before the end of the class, so she went back over the test to make sure she had it correct. A movement over her shoulder had her looking up. Two pieces of paper floated onto the top of her test. It was the map and the timetable the twins had taken from her before the start of lesson. The way it was changed made her grin. They'd marked the Maths Department with a big X and then they'd used different coloured pens to mark out the routes to each of her classrooms. At the top of the map was a colour coded key for the subjects she was taking. They'd even marked where the girls' toilets were, as well as the canteen.

 She turned to look over her shoulder at them. They looked at her and she mouthed thank you, giving them a thumbs up. All she got in reply was a smirk. It made her wonder if they'd tried to mess with her by putting in the wrong routes. She checked the map, tracing the route back to the tutor group. It was marked correctly. So far they weren't misleading her. It would certainly make her life easier until she was more familiar with the layout of the school, and for that she was thankful.

The bell rang to signal end of class, and Mr O'Connor called out for them to try to have a good morning and to do their homework. She got up, grabbed her bag, map, and test papers and made her way down to his desk.

"Sir." She held out the papers to him.

"Excellent, Lily. I'll go through these, and tomorrow we'll know where to kick off from. Where are you headed next?" He took them from her, his eyes already going over her answers.

"English," she said, slinging her messenger bag over her head, freeing the hair that got caught under the strap.

"You know how to get there?"

"Yes, sir, thank you."

"Excellent, off you go then," he said vaguely, his attention solely on her paper. She left the classroom and closed the door. She followed the direction marked on the map, hoping the twins weren't tricking her, and was pleased when she arrived at the correct classroom.

Touch

Lunch time found Lily sitting at the only empty table in the canteen. Her new map had got her there much more quickly than if she had tried to find it before they'd adjusted it for her. It was accurately drawn, and for that she was thankful.

"You called my name."

A boy, about her age, was standing by the table, a tray of food in his hands. He was looking at her expectantly, his head tilted slightly to the side. A pair of wire rimmed glasses sat on his long, straight nose. The bluest eyes Lily had ever seen were behind those glasses, watching her intently. His face was thin, angular, and his cheekbones were pretty hot for a guy. No amount of sucking in her cheeks would give her cheekbones quite like that. His lips pursed slightly, and Lily realised she'd been staring at him. But in her defence, he was gorgeous.

"What?" she asked him, not remembering what he had said to her. Did he want to sit with her? She could go with that.

"I said, you called me; you called my name," he repeated himself. He held an air of authority that made her think he might be on the staff, rather than one of the students. He could be a classroom aide and just look younger than he was.

"I didn't call you." She frowned and looked around her. The students at the other tables were paying no attention to either of them, more interested in their own conversations.

"Yes, you did." He spoke clearly as if there was no doubt in the matter. "I heard you."

"Hey, Nate! Who've you found?" Another boy came over, balancing his own tray in one hand whilst carrying a stack of books in the other. He was about the same age, with dirty blonde hair that looked as if he'd run his hands through it several times. It stuck up at odd angles, the front pushed to one side to stop it falling into his eyes. His eyes were a whiskey brown, warm and filled with a spark of friendliness that had her smiling without even realising it. His face was rounder than his friend's, but he was just as good looking. He was taller by an inch, but he was slightly slouched as he came to a stop beside the boy. She realised that they were both students.

"She called my name," Nate said, not taking his eyes from her.

"No, I didn't," Lily repeated herself firmly. "It must have been someone else, because it wasn't me. I'm new here, and I don't even know your name."

"You can call my name," the other boy said with a wide grin. He plopped into the seat opposite her.

"Matthew." Nate's voice held a tone of censure that Lily didn't understand.

"What?" He sent the other boy a wave of his fingers in dismissal and concentrated on Lily again. "You're beautiful, aren't you? And new. You have to be new here, or we'd be dating already."

Lily snorted with laughter at his words. A few boys had flirted with her before, but nothing serious, just hand holding and end of year dance dates. She'd only been kissed once. Jimmy Price had asked her to the end of year dance in Brighton and stolen a kiss as he dropped her home. The lack of feelings it produced in her left her wholly unimpressed. They'd moved the following week anyway, so she never saw him again, and it didn't upset her.

Nate sighed heavily and sat down next to his friend, setting his tray on the table.

"Matt, are you seriously going to hit on her straight away?"

"You snooze, you lose, Nate. You've been here for a good couple of minutes, and you haven't even got the lovely lady's name." He looked at me. "Which is?"

"Lily Adair."

"Welcome to Heathview College, Lily Adair. So, you want to ask me on a date?" Humour shone in his eyes as he grinned at her. "Because I won't say no if you do."

"No, she doesn't," Nate answered before Lily could even open her mouth.

"Don't answer for my girl," Matt said, and stole a chip from her plate. Lily looked at his plate, he'd taken the lasagne option with no chips.

"She's not your girl," Nate said with a smirk. "She hasn't asked you yet."

"I probably won't either." She knew they were only teasing her, there was no way he could be serious about dating her. He didn't know her at all.

"Told you so," Nate said, opening his can of Coke and taking a sip. She knew he was watching her closely, but she refused to be intimidated by his intense stare.

"She said probably, Nate. And probably means yes in my language."

"That's because you don't speak English, Matt," Nate replied smoothly, making Lily laugh.

Matt took another chip from her plate and she sent him a stern look, but he just winked at her and ate it.

"I'll share my lasagne," he said, after swallowing the chip. The lasagne was shining with grease, and Lily shook her head, grimacing.

"Yeah, it's a toss-up between which food item will kill you quicker," Matt said, poking at his lasagne. "Anyway, where were we? Oh, yes. I know where this is going. You're holding out for me to ask you instead, aren't you?"

"She's not holding out on you, and if she should date either of us, it should be me as it was my name she called," Nate pointed out. There was something in his eyes that sent a shiver down her back. There was a calculating look in them that told her he was not as easy-going as he appeared. He was measuring her up, but what he thought of her she couldn't guess.

"I didn't call your name! It was someone else, or maybe you need to get your hearing checked." She saw his eyebrows lift slightly. He opened his mouth to reply, but before he could say anything Matt spoke up.

"So, what brings you to our humble little town? Apart from summer tourists, we don't get many people coming here."

"My mum has a job here," Lily said, and decided to concentrate only on Matt and not worry about what his slightly strange, but admittedly gorgeous, friend thought.

"Cool. What does she do?"

"She's an artist, she's been commissioned to do a painting of someone's house."

Matt's head went back, and she saw him send Nate a quick look before he was beaming back at her.

"I know who you are! It's my parents who've commissioned her."

"Crowder Manor?"

He jumped to his feet, almost sending his books to the floor, but Nate's quick reflexes saved them.

"Matthew Crowder, at your service!" He executed a small bow and then sat back down. "See? Now it's fate. We're going to date because fate has brought us together."

"I think it was more the advance payment to be honest. I'm not a big believer in fate."

"No?" Matt tilted his head, his whiskey eyes still playful. "Now that's a shame. Here, let me read your palm for you." He held out his hand to her.

"It's a ploy to get you to hold his hand." Nate shook his head.

"One that worked," Lily replied and extended her hand to Matt's, palm upwards. His long fingers caught hers, and it hit her like a bolt of lightning. It hammered into her head, taking over every nerve in her body. She felt her eyes roll back in her head, completely unable to stop herself from jerking backwards, taking the tray with her.

"Shit!"

Matt and Nate reacted instantly but were still unable to stop her from slumping onto the floor. The tray of food went with her, chips covered her as she jerked, her hands curled into tight fists.

"Alright, clear the area!" One of the teachers came over. Nate and Matt shoved the chairs to one side. Lily was motionless, her eyes closed as Matt dropped to his knees beside her. He stretched out a hand towards her, a frown of concern between his eyes.

"Matthew!" Nate knocked his hand away and knelt beside him. He reached out and pushed the hair from her face, her eyelids fluttered slightly and then opened. They were unfocused as she blinked, her breathing was heavy and erratic.

"Boys, give her room. The nurse is on her way."

"I'm okay." Her voice was slurred as she struggled to get to her feet, Nate could see she was more aware now and clearly embarrassed.

A wash of concern flooded through him. He got to his feet and scooped her up in his arms, putting a stop to her weak attempts.

"Get the bags, Matt."

She started to protest, but he shook his head. She couldn't walk, and he didn't want to put her down. She needed him, and he needed to look after her.

"It's okay," he murmured. "I've got you."

She tucked her head into his neck and went limp in his hold; she'd passed out.

"This way, Mr Cohen, please." The sharp voice of Nurse Holden brought his head up. He saw Matt juggling his books and all three of their bags, but there was no way he was letting her go now. Something odd happened here, and he intended to find out what it was. She'd denied it strongly, but he knew she'd called his name.

Fae

Nate crossed his ankles as he leant back on the windowsill of his bedroom. They were all here; Matt and the twins. His brothers through choice, his cousins through blood.

Matt was sitting in the desk chair, spinning it from side to side with his feet. He was lost in thought, staring into space. There was no pushing Matt. When he had something serious to say, he would say it when he was ready. Especially after the day they'd had.

Nate had been shocked when Lily jerked backwards and went down with a bang. It was unnerving, watching her shudder and jerk on the floor, until it stopped almost as soon as it started.

He was watching her face when Matt conned her into holding his hand. The moment they'd touched, her eyes rolled up until all he could see were whites, and then bam, she was down.

He'd scrambled to get to her as quickly as Matt, worry forming deep in his stomach the moment her eyes rolled back in her head. Mrs Sanderson demanded they clear the area. But he didn't even need to think about it. He wasn't leaving her, wasn't backing off; he had to help her. He'd realised the moment he saw Matt stretch out his hand to her what he was going to do. It was a reckless move and one that surprised him. Matt was always the one to make sure that they didn't expose themselves.

She'd come around fairly quickly, but he could easily see she was still completely out of it. She'd tried to get to her feet, obviously embarrassed about the whole thing, but she was physically unable to get up. Again, it seemed totally natural to reach out and scoop her up into his arms. She'd tried to resist, but he wouldn't let her go.

Nurse Holden explained to them it was an epileptic fit and that she'd take over from there. They'd left then, still feeling a little shaken by the whole thing. He knew Matt was stewing over something quietly. Even when they'd met the twins later in the afternoon and told them all about it, Matt kept quiet, letting Nate do all the talking. But Nate knew Matt as well as he knew himself. Matt would talk when he was ready and not before.

Nate knew something odd had happened even before she touched Matt's hand. She'd denied it strongly, but he knew for sure that she'd called his name. He would bring it up with them. Though first he'd wait out Matt, knowing that what he was going to say was important.

"I felt something." Matt stopped swaying the chair abruptly.

"What do you mean?" Josh asked, he was sitting cross legged on the bed. Jake was back to back with him, propping each other up, like identical bookends.

"I don't know. I just felt something." Matt frowned at his knees, hands on the arm of the chair as he began spinning from side to side again. "Like she pulled something from me."

"Pulled something?" Josh looked at Nate before looking back at Matt quickly.

"What do you mean, pulled?" Nate asked, and couched down to sit on the floor. He stretched his legs out in front of him and crossed his ankles.

"I don't know. It just felt like a tugging somehow."

"She pulled your hand as she went back," Nate pointed out.

"Yeah, but it was more like an electric zap," Matt replied.

"Hang on, was it a tug or a zap?" Jake asked, shifting slightly so he could see Matt's face better.

"Are you sure it wasn't just lust?" Josh snorted. "Let's face it, she's fucking hot, man. Those dimples when she smiles make us want to do some pretty sinful things to her."

"Thanks, Josh. I'm not a sixteen-year-old virgin that's subject to my hormones."

"No, you're a soon to be eighteen-year-old virgin subject to his hormones," Jake sniggered and was rewarded with a kick to his foot.

"I'm not a virgin." Matt pulled a face at him. "And I'm not that desperate either!"

"You don't think she's cute?" Jake asked in surprise and looked at Josh over his shoulder. "Just you and me, bro. She's all ours!"

"In your dreams," Nate drawled, and looked back at Matt. "Was it lust?"

"No." Matt flipped off Josh and Jake when they laughed. "I mean, yes, she's pretty, but it wasn't that. It was odd somehow. It felt like the moment her fingers touched mine she was inside my head somehow and it felt like electricity. But as she went backwards, it was a tugging sensation." Matt nodded as he spoke. "Yes, that's how it felt; electricity followed by a tugging."

"Sure she wasn't tugging out your brain?" Jake sniggered.

"He'd need one first," Josh replied, and they fist bumped, laughing together.

"Shut up." Matt rolled his eyes at them.

"There's something else," Nate spoke up, he sat forward from the wall, his hands supporting himself on the floor either side of him. "She called my name."

"Oh, you said that. I thought you were just trying to use some lame ass way to chat her up," Matt said.

Nate snorted and shook his head. "Whatever. Back on track, I heard my name. My full name and it could only have been her who called it."

"What all four of them?" Josh asked in surprise. "Ignatius Quentin Benedict Cohen? Jesus Christ, you couldn't mishear that!"

"No, just Ignatius. I heard it clear as day as I walked over. But how many people even know it, let alone call me that? Apart from my mother," he added dryly.

"I'm sure your mum was drunk when she named you," Jake said through a chuckle.

"Can we please stay on track here?" Matt suddenly snapped, causing them all to look at him. "There's something not right with this girl, and we need to know what."

"Not right?" Jake frowned at him. "What do you mean 'not right'?"

"She flips out when I touch her. She's calling out a name that is a closer guarded secret than the aliens in Area 51, then denying she did."

"Matt, there are no aliens in Area 51," sighed Josh, pinching the bridge of his nose.

"That's not the point," Matt snapped. "And of course there are. But you're not getting it."

"Nurse Holden said it was an epileptic fit," Josh said with a frown. He could see how serious Matt was and straightened up slightly.

"There was no trigger," Matt added. "No flashing lights or whatever's supposed to trigger them."

"Nah, they don't always work that way," Jake said. "Just being overtired can trigger them if they're bad to start with. She's just moved here, first day at a strange place. That's a lot of stress; it could have triggered it."

"But epilepsy doesn't explain how a new girl would know my name was Ignatius," Nate pointed out.

"So what are we saying?" Josh asked, his eyes on Jake's. "She's like us?"

"Maybe," Matt allowed.

"It's a possibility," Nate agreed. "And if she is, then she knew my name somehow and used it to get our attention. If that's the case, what really happened when she touched Matt? What does she want? What's she up to?"

"Do we go to Jonas?" Jake asked, turning to look at Nate; they all did. He was their natural leader and had been for as long as they could remember. They didn't second guess it, they didn't even actively think about it. Nate was the lead and that was it.

"I think we should watch her first. It shouldn't be too hard. She's in the village."

"Derry's Lane. They've rented the middle one, number two, according to Mum," Matt said.

"Great, I'm two streets over. You're not too far." Nate looked at the twins and then Matt. "She might be around your house with her mum sometimes as well."

"Just watch her?" Josh asked. "We can do that."

"We like her; she's nice," Jake added.

"I like her too," Matt admitted. "I don't think she's dangerous, Nate. How can a girl that barely tops eight stone be dangerous against us?"

"Come off it, Matt," snorted Josh. "That's a dumb question. We're Fae. Anyone who isn't, is potentially dangerous. There are even ones like us that are dangerous, you know that!"

"And if she is like us?" Jake asked.

"She'll certainly know what you are." Nate looked at Matt. "She would have picked it up the moment she touched you. It may have even caused the fit."

"Shit." Matt ran a hand through his hair. "So what do we do?"

"There is something else," Nate said, his fingers plucked nervously at the carpet beside him.

"What?" Matt leant forward to get a closer look at his face.

Nate shoved his glasses up his nose. "When she fitted, when she went down," he hesitated, gathering his thoughts. "It was scary, I guess, but there was more. I had to get to her, to protect her, it was such an odd feeling. She's a complete stranger, I don't trust her, but for those few minutes I would have fought anyone who tried to make me put her down. And you"—he looked up at Matt—"reached out to heal her."

"No!" Matt shook his head and then closed his eyes as he realised that what Nate said was right. "Yes, yes. I just knew I had to touch her, to take away her pain," he admitted. "I didn't even think. Not even after, not till you just said it. I would have taken her pain and exposed us all, and it didn't even register."

"Fuck," Josh hissed, and completely in sync, he and his twin turned to face them properly. They leant forward, resting their arms along their thighs. "Do you mean that she's— What are we saying here?"

"We're saying nothing," Nate said and stood up quickly, shoving his hands into the back pockets of his black jeans. "The whole thing could be a huge coincidence. Maybe I didn't hear her say my name. I was so sure though." He let out a huge sigh. "She may just have had a fit due to whatever… I don't know. Maybe it just shocked me into being protective. And Matt," he looked at him, "you feel that kind of thing more than us 'cause of your power. Shit, if we let you, you'd heal every tiny cut we get."

Matt shrugged, rolling his shoulders as he sat back in the chair. "Maybe. I wasn't thinking, that much is clear. I don't know though. I've never tried to heal you when others are around."

"No, but let's face it, we've never witnessed an epileptic fit before. It was quite shocking." Nate sighed again, running a hand through his hair. Strands dropped into his eyes, but he didn't move them.

"So, do we go to Jonas?" Josh asked, once again looking at Nate.

"With what?" Matt threw his hands out. "She had a fit, which may or may not be a regular occurrence for her. We know jack shit about her. And not a lot about what happened. What exactly are we going to say to him?"

"Good point. So we watch her," Jake said. "Get to know her."

"I think it's the best plan so far," Nate agreed. "It might be nothing, it might be something, but I don't trust her yet until I know she's not like us."

"And Jonas?" asked Matt. He clasped his hands together and leant forward on the chair.

"Let's play it by ear; see what we find out about her," Nate said. They nodded in agreement, and he was satisfied with that. They would go to Jonas if it was warranted, but there really was no point in going to see him with the little information they had.

It was several days since they'd seen Jonas last. Now that school had started up again, he would be busy teaching in the local primary. They'd first met Jonas when they were seven and he was teaching their year. Matt found a bird in the playground with a broken wing. Josh and Jake had already discovered they could control animals, so they'd settled the bird quietly in Nate's hands. Matt stroked his fingers over the wing, healing it and giving himself a nosebleed in the process. They hadn't known that Jonas was watching them.

He'd taken them to one side and asked them how they'd done it. Nate stepped up at first, denying everything with the others backing him up. Until Jonas held up a hand, palm upwards, a blue flame dancing on his skin.

It was the first indication that they weren't alone. That the things they could do weren't as freakish as they always thought. Nate was particularly relieved as his own power lay within fire, just like Jonas. Josh and Jake had the ability to calm and direct animals in any manner they wished. Matt was the healer. He could just touch one of them, and whatever scrape or bruise they had, he could fix it. But Matt's power came with a boundary. The bigger the wound or illness he had to fix, the more it took out of him. When they were about eight, Nate fell from a tree and broke his arm. Matt hadn't thought twice about it and healed Nate immediately, but it gave him a chronic nosebleed and made him physically sick. Jonas explained that his gift was rare and came with a price.

Jonas also explained other things too. Things they wouldn't have believed if it hadn't been for their own undeniable abilities. Things that they thought were fairy-tales, he explained were real. He was the one who gave them a name to what they were. They were Fae, Fairies; things that shouldn't exist but did.

Jonas explained that there were others like them. He warned them of what they already knew: that it was safer for them to keep their powers hidden from people. Society wouldn't understand, and the potential for abuse was high. He'd also explained that just as in ordinary people there were good and bad, so it was with the Fae. So they'd kept it hidden from everyone except Jonas and never thought about meeting anyone else like them. Now it seemed there was potentially someone else.

It just remained to be seen if she was like them, and if she was, whether she was dangerous or not.

Different

Lily opened her eyes and sighed heavily. Her headache was finally receding to a point where she could think again. The curtains were shut at her window, trying to keep the room as dark as possible.

She lifted her hand to her forehead and moved the cool cloth that lay there. She vaguely remembered her mother picking her up from college and bringing her home. She didn't always remember the events leading up to a seizure. Sometimes it was vague, hazy recollections, other times she remembered clearly. This time she could remember with clarity the events leading up to the seizure. She remembered talking to two gorgeous boys in the college canteen. They'd been teasing her, and she was fairly sure the one called Matt was flirting with her. She remembered holding out her hand for him to read her palm. The moment he'd touched her, she'd had a seizure. Usually that was the part where the colours swirled behind her eyes in a vivid psychedelic pattern.

But this time was different.

This time there were no colours. Instead, she'd seen images; random things shot through her brain. Flames, faces; faces she recognised as Matt and Nate. She'd seen a watermill by a river and the twins she'd met that morning. There were also faces of people she didn't recognise and places she didn't know. There was a flash of a house she didn't recognise. Nothing that made any sense to her. It felt as if she was looking through a photo album of someone she didn't know.

It unsettled her, maybe even frightened her slightly. She'd never had a seizure quite like it before. She'd never seen anything except colours before. Part of her was worried that it was a significant change in her epilepsy; perhaps indicating something was majorly wrong. She sat up in bed looking at the damp cloth in her hands. If she closed her eyes, the things she'd seen were very clear.

She shook her head to get rid of them and immediately regretted it when the pain behind her eyes sharpened.

She got up slowly and made her way to her bedroom door. As soon as she opened it and stepped out onto the wooden floor of the landing, her mother appeared in her own bedroom door. Her face was pinched with worry and sadness as she came towards Lily.

"Do you need something, Lily?"

"No, I'm okay, thanks. I'm going to take some tablets. It's not so bad now and tablets should stop the rest of it."

"Are you sure, honey? You've only been asleep for two hours." Her mother lifted her hand and touched her forehead gently. Her fingers were cool on Lily's still heated skin.

"Is that all?" Lily was surprised. Usually a seizure knocked her out for hours before she could function enough to walk about.

"It's just gone three, we got back here just before one. Maybe it was a smaller seizure, honey."

"It was different," she admitted, and started to go down the spiral staircase to the living room.

"Different? How?" her mother asked, following closely behind her.

Lily went through to the kitchen at the back of the cottage. There was a small dining area in front of the back door that was just big enough for a small round table and two chairs. She slumped down at the table, resting her head on her folded arms.

"How was it different, Lily?" She got a glass from the cupboard and filled it with water from the tap.

"It's always been colours before," Lily said. She knew that she had to tell her mother, but she was also aware that it would no doubt mean endless trips to more doctors and probably more scans and MRIs.

"And this time?" Her mother set the glass and two tablets in front of her and then sat down opposite.

"It was more like images, pictures." Lily took the tablets with the water. "Thanks." She set the empty glass down and rested her head on her folded arms again, her eyes closed.

"Images? What do you mean images? Pictures?"

Lily frowned at the near panic she could hear in her mother's voice and opened her eyes to peer at her.

"Just random things, places, people. I don't know. It was all jumbled together. None of it made sense. Some of it was people I'd met at college. I think it's probably just stress from the move, Mum."

"People?" Her mother lifted her head slightly, her eyes on the empty glass. "What people? Who did you meet?"

"Just some boys at college. Do you want to get me checked?"

"Boys?" Her mother said it as if she'd said aliens. It made Lily laugh, regretting it instantly as pain throbbed through her skull. She was certain there were tiny people inside her skull, all armed with jack hammers and mining for gold.

"Yeah, Mum. You know, boys." Lily closed her eyes again.

"Why? Why would you speak to boys?"

Lily opened her eyes to look at her mother in disbelief. "What? What do you mean why would I speak to boys? I've been talking to boys since Eric Rundle put that worm down my back when I was five on my first day of school."

Her mother shook her head and flapped a hand.

"Yes, yes, sorry. I just... What were you doing when you had the seizure? Were there flashing lights?"

"No, I was just talking to them. One of them, Matt, is the son of the people who've commissioned you to paint their house."

"Son?" Her mother's voice went up on the word and Lily was beginning to think her mother was having a turn of her own.

"Yeah, Mum, you know, a son. Opposite of having a daughter. Their son. Matthew Crowder. Are you feeling okay? Are you worried about my fit?"

"Seizure, Lilith! You had an epileptic seizure, not a fit!"

Lily winced, and her mother reach forward apologetically. "Sorry, honey, I didn't mean to make your head worse."

"S'alright." Lily took her mother's hand and smiled at her. The tablets were already starting to take the edge off her headache.

"I think it's the stress, Lily. I've moved us twice this summer and that's a lot for anyone." Lily heard the unspoken *let alone someone like you*.

It was true though; it had been a particularly stressful summer. As was her mother's tendency, as soon as school ended she was packing and moving them on. They'd found a flat on the outskirts of Portsmouth, and Lily thought that was it for a year, but then the commission arrived in her mother's P.O. Box and the year became four weeks.

Just days before the start of the new academic year, they'd moved to Trenance. Lily wasn't even sure where all her school records were. Portsmouth, or Brighton, or lost in the postal service never to be seen again. Her mother tried home-schooling her when she was younger, but it was impossible for her to juggle painting and teaching, and when she started to paint, the schooling tended to not get done.

"I was doing so well." Lily sighed heavily. "Longest run yet."

"Don't worry, honey. I'm sure it's just everything catching up with you."

"So you don't want to get me checked up?" she asked.

"I don't think so." Her mother shook her head. "I expect it was a mix of new faces, new places and nerves. Do you feel up to eating yet?"

It was an abrupt change of subject and one which surprised Lily, but she'd had enough for the day and the need for sleep was creeping up on her again.

"I think I'll go up to bed. I don't want to miss college tomorrow."

"Okay, darling. If you need anything, call me."

Lily got up, dropped a kiss on the top of her mother's head, and went back up to her bedroom. She crossed to her window, and sitting on the window seat, she pulled one of the curtains open and slid her window up slightly. She could hear the birds singing and the leaves on the trees as they moved in the breeze. The trees seemed even darker today. She caught a movement at the very edge of the tree line and sat up to look closer. She wondered what wildlife lived in the woods. Rabbits and badgers, maybe foxes and even deer. A sense of excitement filled her; as soon as she could, she would be out there, exploring those woods and the beach that lay behind them. She didn't know much about different types of trees, but she could recognise oak, beech, and horse chestnut. It wouldn't be long before she'd be able to collect chestnuts. There was an open fireplace in their living room; maybe they could roast them. That would be fun.

She watched for a few more minutes, but there were no more movements. She got up, debated closing the curtain, and then decided against it. It would be nice to go to sleep being able to see the sky. If she woke in the night, she would be able to look out at the stars.

Her mother dropped her at college the next morning. Her head was clear, and she felt fine, but her mother insisted on taking her, and Lily didn't mind. It was probably more comfortable than the bus if it was anything like the others she'd ridden over the years.

Her mother was heading over to Crowder Manor to meet her employers, so she dropped Lily off a little early. The college ran a breakfast club for the younger kids, so it was open when Lily got there. She used her map to find her way to all the classrooms she would need that day. A part of her still expected the map to be a trick. So far, each guided line was accurate though, and she was grateful for it. She knew it would only take her a day or two to be completely familiar with the layout and then she wouldn't need the map, but until then she would be glad of it.

When she got to her tutor group, only Mr Peters was there. He let her in, keeping the door open behind her.

"How are you feeling today, Lily?" He sat on the edge of his desk and clasped his hands around one raised knee.

"I'm fine now thanks, Mr Peters." She settled herself into the same seat she'd sat in the day before.

"Nasty thing, epilepsy. One of my wife's cousins has seizures. Grand mal or what they call tonic-clonic seizures now," he said matter-of-factly. "It's a shame with all the advancements of modern medicine they can't cure it. Wendy, my wife's cousin, hers was caused by a car accident; scarring on the brain." He didn't say any more, just smiled kindly at her. She knew he was leaving it open for her to say more or to change the subject if she'd rather, and it warmed him to her.

"I can't remember a time when I didn't get them," she admitted.

"That's tough," he said. "You won't be able to drive, will you?"

"No." She shook her head. "That's frustrating. I was doing really well, hadn't had one for six months, but well…" she faded out, shrugging. There was nothing to be done about it now.

"Well, you didn't miss anything much in History yesterday, first couple of days back in a new academic year are always hit and miss." He got up from the desk and went into the Chapter House. He disappeared inside for a few moments, then came back out with some books in his hand.

"Here you go." He came back over and handed them to her. "That's about all we did yesterday. That and a rundown on what we've already studied."

Lily looked at the two books, one was titled *Russian Dictatorship 1855-1992* and the other one was the British history module, *Rebellion and Disorder Under the Tudors 1485-1603*. She knew her mother had checked to make sure that the same courses were being studied here that she already started in her last college, but it was still a relief to see she didn't have to cram a two-year course into one year.

"I used these textbooks in my last college," she told him, looking up at him.

"Excellent, then you should slot right in with us." He gave her an easy grin.

"Top of the mornin' to ya." An overdone Irish accent caught Lily's attention. She turned to see the twins coming through the door, bags slung over shoulders and wide grins on their faces.

"And to you, Masters Nethercott," Mr Peters said, crossing his arms and grinning at them. Lily couldn't help the laugh that left her lips at the greeting.

A few other students were behind them and Mr Peters stood up, checking his watch. She watched as the twins went to the same desks they were sitting in the day before.

"Hey, Lily, how are you feeling?" Sarah sat down and turned to face Lily. Lily knew that something like an epileptic seizure in the middle of lunch would go around the school like wildfire.

"I'm fine, thanks," she replied. Sarah had a shade of concern in her eyes, but there was also the rank curiosity that most people had.

"I saw Nate Cohen carrying you out yesterday." She lifted her fingers, blew on the tips and then shook them. "He's so HOT!" she announced, fanning herself. "Bet it was nice being carried by him."

"To be honest, I wouldn't really have noticed if it was a six-foot gorilla wearing combat trousers that carried me out." She laughed. "I was just grateful someone did and I wasn't left lying in my plate of chips."

"That must be rough." Sarah leant towards her a little more. "Do you get them often?"

"No, that's the first one in six months, I guess the stress of moving triggered it off. I probably won't get any more for a while. Or at least I hope not."

"Do you take medication?"

Beth sat down, dropping her bag onto the floor. She was chewing gum and fiddling with her phone.

"Robert sent me a text," she said smugly. She looked up and gave Lily a smile. "Hey, Lil."

"Robert texted you?" Sarah turned to face her friend. "He finally texted you? What did he say?"

Lily saw Sarah's interest had swapped from her to her friend and she was glad. She put her history textbooks into her bag and took out her timetable. She had Maths again, followed by History and then Geography.

"Okay, people, phones away, let's make a start," Mr Peters called. When she looked up, the classroom was mostly full. She saw one or two look over at her, but no one else made any comment or reference to yesterday. She hoped it stayed that way.

After registration, there were a few minutes before the bell rang. Lily opened her bag and took out the book she was reading. A shuffling noise came from her right, and she turned to see the twins had swapped out desks with the girls who'd been next to her so that they were now beside her.

"Hey, Lily, how are you feeling today?" one of them asked her quietly. He was leaning on his brother's shoulder to see her better. She studied their faces, but they were blank of emotion. Only their eyes showed a little concern, or at least she thought it was concern.

"I'm much better, thanks," she replied.

"Matt said you took a swan dive onto the floor and ended up with chips all over you," the one leaning on his brother spoke to her.

His twin snorted and shook his head. "He didn't put it quite like that," he retorted.

"Well, it's pretty much how it went," she said, looking between them. "Which of you is which?" She still couldn't see any tells that would help her work out who was speaking. But all she got in reply was a wicked smirk with a wink from them both.

"You need to figure that out, Lily."

"Just call us Nethercott if you get confused. That's what most people do," the other twin added.

"Or get you to wear that orange button badge?" she asked hopefully. The one closest to her snorted and shook his head.

"That makes it much too easy for you," he said. "You'll get a clue this morning as we've got Maths first again."

The bell rang, and she slid her book back into her bag and stood up.

"You know Matt?" It sank in what they'd said.

"Yeah, he's our cousin. So's Nate."

"You're all cousins?"

"Yes, our mothers are sisters," he replied as they made their way through the door and towards the Maths department.

"Are Nate and Matt brothers too?"

"No. There are three sisters; April, our mum; May, Nate's mum; and June is Matt's mum. And no, we're not joking about their names."

"April, May, and June. Your grandparents must have had a good sense of humour." She grinned at them. "They must have had you all at the same time, or thereabouts," she added.

"Nate is the eldest, he's eighteen on the 5th of October, then it's us on the 31st, and Matt's is the 2nd of November."

Lily laughed, falling into step with them easily. "You're Halloween babies?"

"Born just before midnight. Mum was not pleased. She'd been all dressed to go to a party, and we decided to turn up five weeks early."

"So who's older between you?" she asked as they went into the Maths classroom.

"I am." They both spoke in unison, and she laughed in disbelief.

"You can't both be older." She chuckled as she climbed the steps to her seat. They sat behind her again, the rest of the students finding seats and chattering loudly.

"We agreed years ago that the seven minutes he was still kicking his heels inside are irrelevant."

She watched as the other twin pulled the button badge from his jacket and pinned it into place on the black jumper he was wearing.

"Josh," she said quietly, and he looked up under his fringe at her. His eyes sparkled with wicked humour.

"Might be." He smirked, and she rolled her eyes.

"I think you're Josh, and I think you're older." She called them out on what they'd just said.

"Why do you think that?" he asked. "He just said I was younger by seven minutes."

"Am I right?"

"You are," he replied and regarded her with interest. "How did you guess?"

"Just a feeling." She shrugged. "Thanks for the altered map. It helped a lot."

"You are more than welcome, Lily Pad." Josh smirked at her.

"Alrighty! Get settled, everyone. Derivatives won't wait for your social lives, and neither will I!" Mr O'Connor came in, slamming the door behind him. Lily was sure he was still wearing the same clothes from yesterday, and his cardigan was still inside out.

"Open up your textbooks to wherever you left off yesterday and work quietly. Any questions, stick your hands in the air. Lily Adair?" She jumped when he called her name but put her hand in the air. He lifted his finger in acknowledgement and came bounding up the steps, two at a time. His hair seemed to bounce with each step, and she found herself mesmerised by it. That was until he slapped her test from the day before on her desk and leant forward, placing both hands on her desk. He had no concept of personal space, and Lily found herself watching his expressive eyebrows as he got right into her face.

"If you'd gone into that foundation room yesterday, I'd have hauled you in front of the Head today for cheating. One hundred percent, Lily! Well done, well bloody done!" He slapped one hand down in emphasis, making her jump again, shocked at his casual swearing in front of students.

"I'm going to enjoy teaching you this year, Lily, and you're going to enjoy being taught by me. Fantastic job. Right, open your book and get on with it." He turned to go back down the way he'd come, hesitated and looked back at her. "You feel better today?"

"Yes, thank you, sir." It was obviously not just the students who talked, not that it surprised her.

"Excellent, if you fit in here, don't you worry. Just try to fall backwards and not down the steps. Actually. Nethercotts! On your feet, desk either side of her please, gentlemen." He clapped his hands together. She heard them scrape out of their chairs. "If you start to fall, one or the other will catch you, won't you, boys?"

"Of course we will, sir." They spoke in unison, and Lily found herself gaping in surprise. He didn't need to do that; she'd be fine.

"I'm fine, honestly. It was probably a one off. I feel fine. They don't need to move, sir."

"We'll watch her, sir," Josh spoke up, and she looked at him apologetically.

"I don't want to split you up," she said.

"Nonsense. They've been split up since the egg divided in their momma. Work hard, my children. Hand in the air if you get stuck." Mr O'Connor turned and jumped his way back down the stairs. She was left staring at him in utter amazement. He was a breath of fresh air, that much was true.

"Just roll with it," Jake said, opening his book and picking up his pen. "He's a certified nutter, but a complete genius with it. He saw us right last year."

"Did you really get a hundred percent?" Josh asked, and Lily shrugged, opening her own book and notebook.

"I like numbers, patterns." She shrugged again. "Has anyone told him his cardy is inside out?"

"Yep," Josh whispered as the class started to quiet down as they began to work. "He just blinks at you if you mention it."

Lily chuckled, and bending over the textbook, got to work. She wasn't joking when she said she loved numbers and soon lost herself in the work. The rest of class was uneventful. Lily felt herself becoming more settled as the time passed.

History was her next class. The twins had Electronics and that was in one of the buildings outside the main building. They said goodbye to her, and she waved in return.

When she got to the classroom, the rest of the kids were waiting outside to be let in. She moved to the side and leant against the wall. Lily saw the cliques were already formed, and while most smiled at her and said hello, they stayed with the friends they had already made. She didn't expect anything else. She'd learnt long ago that with each new school, it took time to establish anything more than a passing hello. It didn't bother her anymore, and with this being her last year, she wouldn't have to go through it again.

"Hello, Lily Flower. How are you doing today?"

She turned to see Matt coming towards her, a big smile on his handsome face. Another boy was with him, but he broke off and moved to talk to a group of girls.

"Hey, Matt."

"You remember my name." He beamed at her.

"I do, and thank you for helping me yesterday," she said, hoisting her bag higher on her shoulder.

"You're welcome. Okay, now?"

"I am, yes, thanks." She smiled at him and realised that now she was standing, he was a good eight inches taller than her. The twins were taller than her by about six inches. She figured they were probably about five ten, but Matt was six foot easily.

He leant against the wall with her, propping one foot behind him. "You didn't miss much yesterday." He nodded towards the still closed door. "He just handed out textbooks. I didn't realise you're taking History, or I'd have picked them up for you."

"Mr Peters gave me them this morning. But thanks anyway."

"So, a bird has told me you've moved into the village. We all live there so you can catch a ride home with us instead of getting the bus."

"I'll be fine on the bus," she said quickly, surprised he was even offering.

"Yeah, right! You obviously haven't ridden on it yet. Take it from someone who's had to use it for the last six years. I was over the moon when I passed my test and got a car. Honestly, the bus takes forever! It goes around every tiny hamlet known to man before heading into the village. The trip takes ten minutes in the car, forty-five on the bus."

"I don't want to be a pain." She wasn't sure letting him take her home each day was a good idea, no matter how good looking he was or how nice he seemed to be.

"You aren't. But I can guarantee you'll be in pain if you take the bus. What's your last subject today?"

"Geography."

"Damn, none of us are taking that one. It's okay though, we have to pass your classroom to get out. Hang around for us, and we'll take you home."

"Who's we?"

"Me, Nate, and the twins. You know us all anyway now."

"There won't be room," she said, still not sure whether she should take him up on it or not.

Matt snorted with laughter. "Five seater cars, Lily, wonderful invention. Besides, I drive a Land Rover Discovery, there's more than enough room. And I promise not to crash."

"Morning." Mr Peters came down the hallway with an armful of papers and his keys balanced on the top. "Sherrie, get the door, please?"

A tall redhead detached herself from her friends and took the keys from the top.

"Thank you, Sherrie. I have excellent news about our trip this autumn," he announced as she held the door open for him. "Get yourself seated quietly."

Lily held back, knowing that all the desks would have been chosen yesterday. Matt nudged her with his shoulder and indicated for her to follow him. He settled himself at a desk by the window and patted the seat beside him. She looked to see where his friend was, but he'd sat at the back with another girl.

"Good thing no one claimed it yesterday." Matt grinned at her.

"Our first trip this term is going to be relaxed." Mr Peters started to write 'Hamerock House' on the board. "While the house itself is not related in any way to either of our courses, there's going to be some lectures held there and a play. Don't all cheer at once," he added when there was a series of groans throughout the room.

"Permission forms are coming around. You know the drill, folks." He handed a stack of papers to those sitting in the front. "Take one and hand them back. Trip is on the last Friday of the month, the 30th. I need those back at the end of next week at the latest!"

"You gonna be able to go?" Matt asked, waiting for the forms to get to them.

"Probably. You?"

"Yeah." He nodded his head and reached forward for the forms the boy in front was holding out. He took two and handed the rest to the girl behind him.

"Here you go." He handed her one, and she took it to read. It was a standard form. She folded it before putting it into her bag.

Mr Peters clapped his hands for attention, and the class grew quiet

She was conscious of Matt beside her much more than she had been of the twins. She had a desk to herself in maths, but with Matt, the desks were in pairs. She was highly aware of every move he made; every fidget, every cough. But at the same time, she was relaxed with him. It was an odd state to be in, and her concentration suffered.

She was so hyper aware of him that when the bell rang, she flung a quick goodbye at him and made for the door before he'd even got his books away. She was going to have to sort herself out, she couldn't afford to spend the year not concentrating fully because she was aware of him beside her.

"Don't forget, wait for us after last class!" he called out. She sent him a wave but didn't commit herself one way or the other. She wasn't sure what it was about him, but there was something she was hyper sensitive to. Maybe her brain connected him with her seizure and was trying to protect itself. She knew logically he wasn't responsible, but she couldn't help but remember touching his fingers, the jolt of electricity and the subsequent seizure. She dismissed that as ridiculous and headed to her next class. Half of her was expecting him to be there, or the twins, or the other one, Nate. She was split between relief and disappointment when she found a seat and realised none of them were there.

She didn't usually make friends this fast and certainly not with boys. She didn't have an awful lot of experience with boys as more than just passing friends. Yes, there had been Jimmy, but they'd only held hands until he kissed her after the dance. She'd learnt at an early age that trying to build anything more than a passing acquaintance was a pointless activity. It would lead to pain if she let herself get too involved with someone, only to never see them again after she moved.

So far though, Matt and the twins were acting as if they wanted to be friends with her, or at least friendly. The twins were helpful yesterday with their map making skills. Matt was concerned because he'd witnessed her seizure, and he was being kind in offering her a lift home.

The problem was she found all four of them attractive on a physical level. Plus, they were all easy going and seemingly kind. Well, the jury was still out on Nate. But he'd been the one to pick her up; he wouldn't have bothered if he wasn't kind hearted. She'd been embarrassed and her head fuzzy with pain, but on a basic level, being held in his arms made her feel safe. They were all being friendly, and it would be nice to have friends so quickly for once.

French

Lunch time found Lily sitting at the same table as before, but this time she'd brought her own lunch. She'd picked up a carton of juice from the vending machine and was contentedly munching through cheese and pickle sandwiches while reading the book she'd brought with her.

"Lily Flower." Matt sat down opposite her, depositing his tray on the table with a bang. "Not risking your life with the school dinners then. Wise decision."

"Hey, Matt," she said, picking a piece of pickle from the edge of the bread before it could fall off. She popped it into her mouth, looking at his plate. "Health risk? And yet, here you are again, going for the lasagne," she pointed out.

"What can I say? I'm a masochist." He grinned and picking up his fork, he started to eat.

"I'm getting dèjá vu." Nate sat down beside Matt at the table. "If we sit here will it cause a repeat of yesterday?"

"Nate!" Matt smacked him on the arm and then shook his head at Lily. "Ignore him."

She looked at Nate, his head was slightly tilted to one side, his eyes looking at her intently. He didn't trust her, but she had no idea why. Was he ignorant enough to think epilepsy was catching? A ripple of annoyance went down her spine, and she shifted slightly, straightening up.

"If you're that worried, you can sit somewhere else," she said calmly.

"Well"—he clasped his hands together and leant towards her slightly, a strand of black hair fell over one lens, but he didn't move it—"we've been at this school since we were twelve, and through all those years, we've always sat at this table for lunch. So if someone needs to move, I wouldn't say it's us, would you?"

"Jesus Christ, Nate!" Matt cried out, dropping his fork.

Humiliation rushed through her, she got to her feet and grabbed her things. Her cheeks were hot under his stare, but she held his gaze. "I hadn't realised you'd marked your territory for so long," she said. "I'll go before you need to pee on the table to re-mark your scent."

Nate sat back, a muscle worked at the side of his jaw as he continued to watch her.

"Lily, sit down; ignore Nate. He's a total ass sometimes. Nate! You fucking prick!" Matt growled at Nate.

"I was joking," Nate said quietly.

She wasn't sure if he was joking or not, but the calculating look in his eyes told her he was up to something. She didn't need that kind of hassle, no matter how good looking he was, or how he'd helped her yesterday.

"I wasn't." She started to move away.

Matt jumped to his feet and blocked her way. "Sit down, Lily, there's nowhere else now anyway," he said gently. She knew he was right. All the tables were taken; it was the reason she'd sat there. She hadn't realised she'd sat at their table the day before, and she'd mistakenly thought it wouldn't hurt if she sat there again.

"Look, I've been in enough schools to know how it works," she told Matt. "There's groups, cliques, and you've all got your own spots. I get it, I'll find somewhere else; this is your table."

"Lily, please." He hesitated slightly before reaching out to put his hands on her shoulders. "Sit down."

"Sit down, Lily. He's right; I was being an ass." Nate caught her attention. "I apologise. It started out as a bad joke and went wrong. You're welcome to sit at this table, I'll even pee over you, if you want."

It would be better for her to walk away. To avoid getting too friendly with them.

"Please, Lily. I was being an ass." She caught his eyes and saw the contrition in them. He helped her yesterday, and she hadn't thanked him yet.

"I'll sit down." She slid back into the chair. "But I think I'll pass on the peeing, thanks."

"Your loss," he said with a shrug, and then did the unthinkable and smiled at her. It was a proper smile that started on his lips and ended in his eyes. She found herself smiling back at him.

"Thank you for carrying me out yesterday." She kept eye contact with him. "You didn't have to do that, but I'm grateful you did." She watched as something seemed to thaw inside him and his whole posture relaxed slightly. He hadn't trusted her, she just had no idea why though.

"You're welcome, Lily." He smiled.

His eyes held hers, and Lily felt herself relax; he really did have lovely eyes. She'd never understood what it meant to get lost in someone's eyes, but now she did.

"What've we missed?"

The twins stopped at the table, trays in hand and bags over shoulders. They looked as if they'd been outside as their hair was windswept and falling into their eyes.

"A pissing contest," Matt said, his mouth full. "Lily won, I think."

"I think she did," Nate agreed, and held out a hand to her to shake. "Let's start again. I'm Nate Cohen. Nice to meet you, Lily Adair."

"Nice to meet you, Nate." She reached out her hand, grinning at him. She shook his hand firmly and then let go to pick up her sandwich. His grin widened and he seemed satisfied over something, but what it was Lily had no idea.

"What did you mean 'enough schools you've been too'?" Matt asked.

"We move a lot," she said casually.

"You and your mum?" asked one of the twins. She looked up at them and nodded. They were eating chips with their fingers, cans of Coke on their trays, and she suddenly saw it.

"Josh?" One of the twins looked up a split second before the other one did, but it was enough.

"What?" He took a swallow of his Coke.

"You're mirror twins," she said, and they looked at each other in surprise before looking back at her and grinning.

"We are." Josh tipped his Coke at her in acknowledgement. "What gave it away?"

"You're opposites. You're right handed and Jake is left. You're using opposite hands to each other. It's why you're so like each other. I've met twins before, but there was always a slight difference facially, but you two? Mirror images of each other."

"Yup. Right down to the mole on our hips," Josh said.

"So even your bodies are mirror imaged?"

Jake winked at her and leant forward slightly. "Yeah, and if you're really lucky, Lily, we'll let you see those moles one day."

"Jake!" Nate shook his head, rolling his eyes. Lily hid her blush by bending to put her book into her bag.

"It used to be a pain," Josh spoke up. "Being opposite handed didn't serve us well when we wanted to fool people, so he learnt to write right handed and I learnt to write left handed. We can use either hand now and our writing is the same."

"It's pretty rare, isn't it?" she asked.

"We're special," Josh said, a wicked smirk curled his lip.

"Oh you're special, alright," Matt teased. In perfect sync they both flipped Matt off, making Lily shake her head in amazement at how together they were. They really were like one person split in two.

"Lily?" Matt caught her attention as she finished off her sandwich. "How often have you moved?"

"I can't remember a time when we weren't moving," she said with a shrug. "I can usually make it to the end of an academic year, and then when summer rolls around we move. Mum paints, and she's always chasing the next picture I guess."

"Shit. You mean you move every year?" Nate asked, surprise in his eyes and face.

"Yeah. I know it sounds odd, but it's just how it's always been."

"So, let me get this right," Jake spoke up and she looked over at him as she opened her carton of juice. "You finish a school year and then move somewhere else?"

"Yeah, it was a bit odd this time though. I finished up in Brighton and we'd moved to Portsmouth, but then your parents," she looked at Matt, "got in touch with Mum and we moved the following week to... well, here."

"You moved twice in the summer holidays?" Matt snorted. "No wonder you had a seizure yesterday. I think I'd have one if I had to move that quickly."

She was suddenly aware that all four of them were looking at her, identical looks of pity mingled with surprise in their eyes. She didn't like the pity, but it was something she saw every time she told someone how often she'd moved.

"It's not so bad," she said. "I've never minded. I'm used to it."

"It must make your head spin," Matt said, shaking his head. "You don't know whether you're coming or going."

"Sure I do," she replied. "I've never known anything different. I'm okay with it. I love seeing new places, meeting new people."

"But you can't put roots down," Josh said. "What about your family?"

"Mum's the only family I have. My dad died when my mum was still pregnant with me."

"No brothers or sisters or other family?" Matt asked, and she shook her head.

"Just me and Mum." She smiled at him. "It's not nearly as bad as it sounds. I've visited more places in this country than most people have. I've lived in Scotland, Wales, a lot of places in England, and now I'm in Cornwall."

"But what if you find a place you really like? A place you really want to stay in and not leave?" Jake asked, taking a chip from Josh's plate as his own was now empty. She noticed Josh didn't say anything, just pushed the plate slightly closer to Jake.

"I've never been anywhere that has made me feel that way," she admitted. "Mum has always tended to stay in cities or towns. This is the first place that's been out of town."

"And do you like it here?" Nate asked her. She watched as he separated his peas from the rest of his mixed vegetables, and pushed them to the edge of his plate.

"I've only been here a few days, but I like it so far. Our cottage is pretty."

"You're down on Derry's Lane," Matt said, polishing off the last of his lasagne. Nate picked up his plate and pushed all his peas onto Matt's plate. Again, nothing was said. It was such an intimate act that Lily was beginning to see just how close they all were.

Matt began to eat the peas as Nate carried on with his cottage pie. Lily picked at the skin on her apple. Something about the way they were with each other sent a pang of longing through her. She was close to her mother, had always been close. She'd had friends of a sort, but she'd never had a relationship with a friend that was more than casual, and none that ever offered to keep in touch with her. She'd never had a best friend, and it hadn't bothered her. But there was something about these four that she wanted for herself. She wanted that informal connection with someone. She wanted someone to know her better than she knew herself, and to know someone that well in return.

"Those are old worker cottages," Matt spoke up again. "There's an old quarry just outside of the village. Disused now, but there's a pool in the old quarry that's safe to swim in."

"But don't go there alone," Nate spoke up suddenly. "It's deep, and there's only one exit point. If you got into trouble on your own, no one would know."

"We go down most weekends. Want to come with us this Saturday?" Josh asked her. He began stacking his and Jake's plates on the trays.

His question took her by surprise, and she felt a longing to join in.

"Sometimes the other village kids go there as well," Matt added. "It's more popular than the swimming pool in town. Free as well."

"Yes, okay. I'd like that. Don't worry if you decide you can't make it though," she said. She wanted to go with them, wanted the chance to make friends with them. She realised that they were already a unit, and being boys they wouldn't be looking to make her their new best friend, but she didn't need that. She just wanted some friends for as long as she was here.

"We'll make it," Nate said. "We'll come around for you just after lunch, gives the water chance to warm up a bit. Although, I'll warn you now, it's colder than river water. It's going to get too cold to swim in it soon."

"Understatement, Nate," Jake retorted. "It's freezing; it will take your breath away when you jump in."

"Will that affect your epilepsy?" Matt asked, he leant forward slightly, his whiskey coloured eyes intent on her.

"I wouldn't think so," she said with a shrug. "I've been swimming in cold river water before."

"What does trigger it?" asked Josh.

"I take medication, so I'm usually okay. But I guess it's the usual: stress, being overtired. I was doing okay. I haven't had one for six months."

"What's it like?" asked Matt, and then waved a hand apologetically at her. "No, sorry, that's a personal question."

"It's okay. I don't mind talking about it. Invariably people ask when they find out anyway."

She set her apple core on her plate. "It's weird I guess. I don't get a warning or anything. I just suddenly go down."

"Has it ever happened like that before?" asked Nate. They were watching her intently, and it made her want to slink down in her chair. It was like they were hanging onto every word she said, as if it held the answer to mankind's problems, and not just her boring life. It was intimidating.

"What do you mean?"

"Has someone's touch ever sparked it off before?" Jake clarified for her.

Her head went back, and she stared at him before looking at Nate. "Matt didn't cause it. Is that what you thought?" Had she done something to make him think it was him that caused it? Maybe her attitude in class had made him think it. She had shot out of there very quickly. She winced, feeling bad.

"It just seemed odd," Matt said, an easy-going smile on his face that didn't quite reach his eyes.

"Bad timing." She sat forward making sure he was looking at her. "It really was just utter bad timing. It's happened before. I was at a fairground last summer, queueing to go on the carousel. I paid my money to the guy, he gave me the change and bam, I was down. Fortunately, Mum was with me and they had St. John Ambulance there as well. It really doesn't have a rhythm or reason to it. I don't know why it happened then either. I don't have photosensitive epilepsy. Lights don't seem to affect me, it really is random. But it was definitely not you, Matt."

"What does it feel like?" Matt asked.

"Usually it's just like a lot of swirling colours before I lose consciousness and then I'm back again, feeling as if a ten-ton truck has run me over."

"Usually, so, not always?" Nate asked. She looked at him, her eyes caught his, but all she could see was mild curiosity.

"Well, I guess." She shrugged again, there probably wasn't any harm in telling them what happened this time. She was certain it was just the added stress from moving twice in such a short space of time. "This time was a bit different. I didn't get the colours, I just got a load of random things." She picked at the apple core, pulling out the seeds.

"Random things?" Jake asked, he was looking up at her from under his fringe.

"Well, you, I saw all of you, places, just random things. I think most of it was jumbled up because I was overtired, and a little bit stressed from the move."

"And have you seen anything like that before?" Nate asked, and once again she had the feeling her answer was important to him.

"No, but they have changed over the years. I didn't get tonic-clonic seizures until I was about twelve, before that I had absence seizures."

"Absence?" asked Jake with a frown. "What's that?"

"For a couple of seconds I just used to blank out, stare into space, but I didn't know I was doing it." She set her seeds into a star shape on the tray. "But I can tell you now one hundred percent, Matt, that it was not you. You may be nice, but you're not seizure inducing." She smiled at him, desperate for him to know it wasn't his fault.

"Damn, I thought I'd made such an impression on you that I just swept you off your feet into a good old fashioned swoon."

Relief swept through her, and she held out both hands. "No, none of you will make me swoon if you touch me; go ahead, I'll prove it."

"Ah, shit, Lil, way to stamp on a man's ego," Jake pouted, his bottom lip trembled, but his eyes sparkled.

"I'm quite sure you have enough of the female population here swooning over you already," she said with a wink. "You don't need me adding to it."

"Maybe we do," Nate said. He reached forward and gripped her hands in his. His fingers were long and slim with clean nails. She liked the feel of them, but there were no blinding lights and she hadn't expected any.

"Nothing, I'm afraid." She looked at the twins. "Want to play Russian roulette?"

Nate let go of her hands with a laugh. Josh and Jake reached over and took a hand each, and as before, nothing happened. Their grip was firm, and she could see they bit their fingernails.

"Nada," she said with a laugh. She looked over at Matt. "Wanna try it again?"

He grinned at her, reached out and took her hand from Josh. He brought it towards him and kissed the back of her hand. She laughed, her other hand still held in Jake's. She felt him tug her his way and then his lips were on the back of her hand.

"Hey, guys, enough." She laughed, her cheeks firing up again. "You'll make me swoon."

"That's what we were aiming for." Jake chuckled, and leant back in his chair putting his arm over the back. Josh leant forward, snapping his fingers at her.

"Come on, hand, please," he commanded. "Nate, we can't let these two one up us."

"Not likely." Nate smirked and held his out to her as well. She lifted her hands, laughing as they kissed the backs of her hands. Nate kept his eyes on hers as he bent over her hand, and she couldn't stop the laughter that spilled from them teasing her.

"Boys, boys, you have no idea where these hands have been." She chuckled, trying to get them to let her hands go, but they were holding fast.

"I'm sure you know how to use soap and water," Nate said with a grin. "It smells like it, anyway."

"Can I have them back now?" They loosened their hold, and she pulled her hands free, grinning at them.

The overhead bell rang, and Matt got up immediately. He picked up her rubbish and put it on his tray.

"I can take it," she protested.

"I know you can, but I'm still working towards a swoon from you, don't spoil it."

She picked up her bags and stood up, thanking him. She liked them, she liked them a lot. There was a false start with Nate, but he seemed easier with her now. They were friendly, funny, and they seemed to have accepted her. She knew better than to get too involved with any of them, but she would enjoy their friendship for as long as she was here. And when it came time to move on again, she'd say goodbye and take with her some good memories. If she didn't make the kind of connection they shared, then it would be for the best.

"What've you got next?" Josh asked as they left the canteen.

"French."

"I'm taking French too," Nate said and fell into step with her. "I'll walk with you."

The others were heading to different subjects, and she said goodbye to them before heading down the corridor with Nate. Now that she was alone with him, she felt a little nervous, wondering if perhaps he was friendly with her for the others.

"What do you have planned for Uni?" he asked as they arrived at the still closed door. There were several students already there, and she recognised a few faces from her Maths class.

"I don't know yet," she replied, leaning against the wall.

"Hello, Nate," came a breathy voice. She saw a pretty girl with long flame coloured hair coming down the corridor. She wore the college uniform of black skirt, white shirt, and black tie with the college crest on it, same as Lily did. Somehow, this girl managed to make it look sexy.

"Connie." He nodded his head at her but made no move to say anything else to her. Connie looked at Lily and tilted her head.

"You're new?"

Lily nodded at her. "Just moved in."

"Let me warn you about Nathan Cohen then. He's a heartbreaker, aren't you, Nate? They all are, that lot."

"Connie, leave it," he said. Lily watched with interest. Connie shrugged and looked back over her shoulder to where her friends were gathered.

"Whatever. Say hi to Matt for me," she said and turned to go back to her friends.

Lily looked at Nate. A small muscle worked on the edge of his jaw, and his eyes were hard behind his glasses. He was watching Connie as she leant against the wall turning her back to him. She couldn't see any signs of anger, or pain in his eyes, but she had an idea that she had been his girlfriend at some point. Whatever it was, it was none of her business.

"Your full name is Nathan?" she asked him. He turned his head without moving his body, and those blue eyes were focused on her.

"Is that all you want to know from that conversation?" he asked.

"I think it's probably none of my business, not even your name really." And it wasn't. She might want to be their friend, but that didn't give her access to everything about them.

He relaxed his jaw line, and the muscle tick stopped. "She's Matt's ex-girlfriend. And no, Nate is not short for Nathan." He gave her a small grin that she returned without even thinking about.

"Nathaniel?" she asked as the door opened, and the teacher indicated for them to go inside.

"Nope, now shut up, Lily Adair, and come sit with me. There's a free seat next to me."

Lily followed him to the back of the classroom and sat down at the shared desk. For some reason, none of them had buddied up. The twins were together obviously, but there was no one sitting next to Matt, and now it seemed as if Nate also had an empty seat beside him. This was their second year of A levels in already established classes, so it was logical to assume that last year they hadn't been paired with anyone either. She couldn't help but wonder why.

"Calme, s'il vous plaît, mesdames et messieurs. Tous les téléphones loin ou ils seront confisqués."

There was a rustle as mobiles were put away into bags.

"She's not joking either," Nate murmured. "She'll confiscate it if she sees it. Which reminds me, on the way home we'll swap out phone numbers." He kept his voice low as he spoke, his eyes on the small petite woman that was their French teacher.

He wanted her number and was going to give her his. That was a first for Lily. She'd never swapped out phone numbers with people before. She'd never needed to. She had one contact number on there and that was her mother. She'd never even thought about it before. There'd never been a need to have someone else's number on her phone. She wondered briefly if she was going to make things difficult for herself when it came time to say goodbye.

"Miss Adair, welcome to my class. This will be your textbook for the year. I'm Madame Fontaine, any questions, please ask." She stopped beside Lily's desk and held out the book to her.

Lily took it and looked up at the small woman. Her straw coloured hair was pulled into two braids on either side of her face, her skin was wrinkled with age, but she looked pleasant and her faded blue eyes were kind. She was dressed as if she needed to wear every colour of the rainbow at the same time, but in a weird way, it worked. She was unique.

"*Merci,* Madame Fontaine," she said, and received a wide smile in return.

"*Bien.*" She went back to the front of the class.

Nate nudged her arm gently. "I think I've just found a way we can wind up Matt and the twins." His smirk was wicked. "They're useless at French."

"Ohhh, mean," she whispered back, grinning.

"But satisfying," he said and sat back in his seat, pushing his glasses up his nose and focusing on Madame Fontaine as she started the lesson.

Lily felt a spark of warmth slide through her. Normally at this point in the year she was still trying to fit in. She wouldn't know anyone and would still be sitting on her own and eating on her own at lunchtime. It usually took a few weeks, if not months, before she was included in any established friendships.

But this year? This year was looking far better than any before.

Aye!

The final bell of the day rang, and Lily slid her books into her bag. She groaned when she put it over her head. Now that she had all her textbooks it was heavy. She debated whether she might be better off buying a backpack to make it easier to carry. But she liked her messenger bag. It was a pale grey colour, and she'd decorated it with permanent markers. Each year, for the past six years, she'd added somewhere on the bag the crest of whichever school she was in. Before the year was up she'd add the *Heathview* crest. As crests went, it would be an easy one to draw. It was three blue wavy lines with an anchor above them, *Heathview College* in script above it, and *Noli Cedero Cognoscere* under it. She didn't know what the Latin meant, but the boys would probably know.

She stopped outside the classroom door, standing to one side to avoid the rush of students. Matt had told her to wait for them and they'd give her a lift home, but there was no sign of them yet. She had no idea where their classrooms were in relation to hers. She just knew that Matt told her they passed this room. But what if they'd forgotten her? They might be friendly in class and at lunch times, but there was no reason why she would stand out enough for them to really bother with her. She checked her watch; there were ten minutes before the bus would leave, stranding her here. She would wait for another couple of minutes and then move on. She'd rearrange her bag, and then when they didn't turn up it would just look like she was sorting her bag to make it easier to carry, and not that she'd been stood up.

Stood up?

It was a car ride home, not a date. She crouched on the floor pulling her books out of the bag, irritated with herself. She may have found them attractive physically, but that didn't mean they liked her that way. All they'd offered was a car ride, and here she was acting as if they'd asked her on a date. And if they did ask her, which they wouldn't, how could she pick between them anyway? She huffed her breath out in annoyance, stuffing her books back into her bag. Now she was being ridiculous, why would she have to choose when there was no likelihood of them liking her that way? She knew Matt had flirted with her, but that was before she'd flipped out on him and he saw what a mess she was. Epilepsy was exhausting, not just for the person who suffered from it, but for the person who cared for them. She couldn't be left alone for long; she couldn't drive; she couldn't even take a bath unless her mum was in the house and even then she had to leave the door open. Why would anyone willingly want to take that on? Who would want to take her on?

She got up, completely annoyed with herself. She never allowed herself to wallow in self-pity. Her mother never allowed her to feel sorry for herself. She had epilepsy, she wasn't dying. She shouldered her bag and checked her watch. She could wait for five minutes or she'd miss the bus, and there was still no sign of them. The corridor was empty of other students as well now. She ruthlessly shoved down the feelings of disappointed hurt and walked away.

She got as far as the main entrance when she heard her name being called. A rush of relief went through her when she recognised Matt's voice. They hadn't forgotten her. She stopped and looked back. They were coming up behind her, the four of them in a row. She sucked in her breath. Individually they were good looking, as a unit they were gorgeous eye candy. She shook her head and shouldered her bag again, she would not embarrass herself by drooling, she was sure that the stupid grin on her face was doing that job for her already.

"Did you forget?" Matt asked as they drew level with her. He reached out and took her bag, slinging it over his own shoulder. She moved to take it back, but he frowned at her.

"I'm still trying to get you to swoon!" Matt mock scolded her. "Let me at least pretend I'm a gentleman."

"Why didn't you wait?" Nate caught her attention, and she decided to be honest.

"I thought you'd already gone," she admitted. She saw the frown between his eyes, but he said no more and started to walk forwards.

"And leave you behind?" Josh exclaimed and slung his arm around her shoulder. "Lily Pad, how could you think that of us? I'm highly offended." They began walking out of the front entrance and down to the carpark, but Josh didn't move his arm and Lily didn't mind.

"How was Diggers?" Jake asked, walking backwards in front of her. "Does he still chuck the board eraser if you muck about?"

"I haven't found that out yet; no one mucked about today. But I'm debating mucking about just to find out now." She grinned as she thought of her Geography teacher, Mr Digby, throwing board erasers around the room. He was an imposing figure of a man. Tall and heavyset, with a black beard that made her think of pirates. He wore a three-piece suit with a gold chain pocket watch. His obvious devotion to his subject made him fascinating to listen to, and she'd enjoyed his class a great deal.

"Don't!" Nate warned. "He has excellent aim."

"He chucks it at the person? How does he get away with that?"

"This is backwater Cornwall, Lil. They only stopped using the cane last year, and that was because it broke from overuse on the twins," Matt said and dodged the thump Jake sent his way.

They came to a stop by a Land Rover in gunmetal grey. It was an older model, mud sticking to the sides and the tyres. Matt stopped by the driver's door, his eyes on her bag.

"Are these all the crests from the schools you've been in?" Matt looked up at her. There was that tiny glint of pity in his whiskey eyes, and it irritated her.

"Yeah, this place will go on there. Oh, by the way, what does the motto mean?" She pushed down the irritation.

"Don't cease to learn," Josh answered her. They all gathered around Matt, looking at the different crests she'd drawn. "Are you taking Art here?"

"No." She shook her head.

"You should, these are really good!" Josh pointed to the crest of Hogwarts that she'd drawn. "Although, I don't think you went there, did you?"

Lily laughed and shook her head. "No. That's the only one I want to go to though."

"You do know it's not real, don't you?" Nate teased her.

"Don't tell me that." She pouted. "I've been telling myself that my owl just keeps getting lost."

"For six years? It's not lost, Lil, it's dead," Josh said as he came towards her. "C'mon, Lily Pad, front seat for you." He opened the passenger door for her. She grabbed the handle, put her foot on the step, and hoisted herself up and into the seat.

"I was wondering if you'd make it, or if I'd have to throw you in." Josh chuckled, closing the door and getting into the back with Jake and Nate.

"Whose seat have I nicked?" she asked, putting her belt on and turning to look back at them. It was quite spacey inside and they weren't squashed together, so she felt better about taking the front seat.

"It's a free for all, Lily; a violent, messy, free for all," Matt drawled. "I have witnessed blood being shed as those three try to get to the front seat before each other."

"I slipped on the ice!" Jake defended himself. "I grabbed Nate to stop my fall."

"You shoved me, and it backfired on you!" Nate snorted.

"Well, none of you reprobates have to worry about shoving again, and I won't have to worry about blood on my seat covers. That seat is now officially Lily… What's your full name, Lil?"

"Lilith May Adair."

"Lily May?" Nate sounded it out. "I like it."

Matt joined the queue of buses leaving the carpark. There were six buses and they were all turning left onto the main road, building up a queue.

"Lilith? You're a night monster," Josh sniggered.

Lily looked back at Josh laughing. "I prefer Storm Goddess, actually," she said with a grin, referring to what her name meant in its original Hebrew.

"Yeah, so do I," Matt said and looked at her sideways, catching her eye. "You're a Goddess, Lily. Never a monster."

"Ah, but you don't know me yet," she teased him, covering the pleasure his words gave her. She lifted her hands making claw shapes with her fingers. "I could be anything at all."

"Why don't you tell us what you are?" Nate asked, and although his voice was light, she heard an edge of something she couldn't place. She turned to look back at him. He was sitting in the middle seat.

"I'm just me," she said, holding his gaze. She had the feeling that he was searching for something, an answer she didn't even know the question to.

"When are you eighteen, Lil?" Jake asked her.

"End of September." He rolled his finger indicating he wanted more information. "Twenty-ninth," she added.

"We'll celebrate by taking you to the Bootlegger," Matt said.

A ripple of excitement through her that they wanted to celebrate her birthday with her.

"The what?" She tried for casual, but her heart was going a mile a minute.

"The pub in Trenance. It's only a small pub that locals use, but it's a nice place."

"You're not eighteen yet," she pointed out.

"It does pub grub as well. Besides, you'll be able to drink. It's a rite of passage, turning eighteen and buying your first drink in a pub with friends," Jake said.

"We'll pay," Matt said. "C'mon, Lil, your eighteenth is a landmark. We can't just let that slide. Couple of days later we'll be celebrating Nate's. Josh and Jake are next month, and mine's November. We're all doing it."

She clenched her hands in her lap and bit her lip. Her birthday was always just her and her mother. It fell close to the start of a new school year, so she'd never known anyone long enough for them to ask when her birthday was. It hadn't bothered her. She got invited a couple of times through the years to birthday parties of others, but she never imagined having anyone to celebrate her birthday with. But here they were, telling her that they wanted to do something for her birthday; that she should celebrate with friends. Which meant they viewed themselves as her friends. They were worming their way in quickly. When she moved at the end of the year her heart wasn't going to just break, it was going to shatter.

"What are you thinking, Lily May?" Nate had leant forward between the seats, his mouth close to her ear sent a shiver down her back.

"I won't be staying here." The words were out before she even had time to think about them.

"But you're here now," he said softly. He put his hand on her shoulder briefly, then he sat back. "It's decided. The Bootlegger for a birthday bash for Lily May. All in favour, say aye."

A chorus of 'ayes' went up loudly, and then Matt was looking at her. "Come on, Lily Flower, let's hear your aye or nay. It's compulsory to vote, but I would just add that you're already outnumbered, so if you vote nay it'll just be a waste of breath."

Lily shook her head, a smile on her lips. He was right; she was here now, there was no point in worrying about next year until next year. A warm bubble sat in her chest, making her feel lightheaded, and she knew what is was: happiness.

"Aye!" she said.

A roar of approval went around the car, and she was completely unable to keep the smile from her lips.

Matt finally pulled onto the main road and turned right instead of left. "We'll be home much quicker this way," he said, reaching forward to the car stereo. A popular song blasted out of the speakers, and he turned it down slightly.

"You okay with this?" he asked her.

"Yes, it's fine."

Josh and Jake were already starting to sing along loudly. She wound her window down enough for the wind to catch her hair, sending it flying around her face. She heard Nate and Matt join in, and with a nudge from Matt, she started to join in, too. She couldn't sing, but then neither could Josh and Jake and it didn't stop them. Content to sing quietly along, she leant her head back against the headrest, her eyes on the scenery as they sped down the winding country lanes towards Trenance.

Trenance was really a collection of five streets that all went out from a central typical English village green like spokes on one side of a wheel. The lane she lived in was the only road in and out of the village. All the other lanes were cul-de-sacs, ending at either the woods or fields. One of the lanes held the pub and the shops, and the other lanes held cottages identical to hers. The green in the middle of the village had a stream fed duck pond, flowerbeds and several benches under the trees that dotted around. It was quintessentially British, the type of place that made excellent postcard pictures, or jigsaw puzzles. A war memorial surrounded with red paper poppies and black railings sat on the edge of the park. To the edge of the green was an old fashioned, red telephone box, its only nod to modernisation was the sticker on the top that declared it took card or coins. Matt pulled in beside it, keeping the engine running.

"Have you got your phone, Lily May?" Nate asked her. She turned, remembering he wanted her number.

"It's in my bag." She took her bag from Josh when he held it out for her. "Thanks." She opened it and took out her phone.

"Is that contract?" Matt asked, digging out his own.

"No, it's pay as you go. It's hard getting contracts when we move so much." She scrolled through the phone to her contact list to find her own number.

"Tell us your number," Nate instructed her. "We'll call it, and you can save our numbers that way. Okay?"

Lily nodded and began reading out her number. From the corner of her eye she could see Nate and the twins also putting it into their phones.

"Matt, you go first," Nate commanded. Lily's phone rang in her hand, and she only just stopped herself from answering it.

"I'm not sure how to add it," she revealed, when she found the number in her call log. She had put her mum's in, but it was a while ago now and she couldn't remember how she did it.

"Here." Matt's long, slim fingers plucked the phone from her, then he leant across holding it so she could see the screen. "In here, in your call logs. Press the cross button and then it takes you to contacts. Put in my name…" He tapped away, and she saw Marvellous Matt appear in the name section. She snorted with laughter and then saw him save it, the number appearing there as well. "There you go. Nate, go for it. You do it this time, Lily Flower." Matt handed it back to her as it began to ring.

She did as he showed her and put in Nate Cohen and then saved it. Nate's hand appeared between them and the phone was taken from her. She heard him tapping on the screen and then he was passing it back. Nate the Great had replaced Nate Cohen.

"Uh, uh," Josh objected and once more it was taken. "We get to put our proper names too," he said and she turned to see his fingers flying over her screen. Jake was leaning over Nate, looking down at the phone, the side of one thumb nail was between his teeth.

"Posh Josh and Fake Jake? Fuck you, Joshua!" He shoved Josh and then snatched her phone from him. He tapped quickly before handing it back to her. She took it, her cheeks were beginning to hurt from smiling so much. She looked down at her contacts and saw Jake had put their names as Sexy Jake and Loser Josh.

"That doesn't even rhyme, you idiot." Josh shoved Jake and a scuffle broke out between them, reaching across Nate, who wasn't impressed.

"Children! Pack it in or you'll walk home!" he ordered.

"We are home, Dad," Josh sniggered.

"Derry's Lane is that one." Matt pointed to the lane behind her. "Josh and Jake are opposite, past the green, in Hangman's Lane. Nate is over there in Toll Lane," He pointed to the other side, "and

I'm just out of the village in the old vicarage. My place is a fifteen-minute walk from the bottom of your lane. Ten if you nip through the woods." He turned to look back at the others. "Instead of here, let's change it to outside Lily's," he said and they agreed. "We'll pick you up tomorrow at eight outside yours, Lily Flower."

"Thank you. It's kind of you," Lily said honestly.

"Not really," Matt replied and smiled at her.

"Who's that?" Jake asked from the back. Lily and Matt turned to look at Jake, he was frowning, looking out of his window in the direction of Lily's lane. "He's not a local. Just came out of the middle cottage."

Lily turned in her seat and saw a car door close before whoever it was pulled off and headed out of the village. "I don't know." She shrugged. "We're in the middle one, maybe it was the landlord."

"Matt's dad is the landlord," Jake spoke up. "And that was nothing like his dad."

"Your dad is my landlord?" she asked in surprise, turning back to Matt.

"He's the Lord and Master around here," Josh sniggered and Lily saw a blush cross Matt's cheek, and then he was flipping Josh off over his shoulder.

"Don't be a moron," Matt sneered.

"He is!" Jake spoke up. "Master Crowder of Crowder Manor. Owns most of the rented property in the village."

"I thought it was a vicarage," Lily said to Matt.

"It is, or rather it was. But it's very old and now it's called Crowder Manor. Locals still call it the vicarage though."

"So your dad's not the vicar then?" she asked and he laughed, but she heard an edge to it.

"No, not the vicar," he replied. She heard Nate snort in derision behind her and figured she was stepping onto a sore subject.

"Well, I'd best be getting on home, but thanks again." She reached for the door handle.

"Is your mum home?" Josh asked.

"I'm a little early." Lily looked at her watch. "She said she'd get in when the bus did. It's no problem, I'll get some homework done. See you tomorrow and thanks again."

She slid from the Land Rover, her bag in her hands and heard the other doors opening and closing.

"See you tomorrow, Lily Pad." She heard the twins call to her as they jogged off in the other direction. Nate shut his door and turned to her.

"I'll walk you," he said, and there was no room for argument in his voice.

She waved as Matt pulled off and then turned to Nate. "You're the other way."

"Jesus, Lily May, it's all of three lanes away. Hardly miles." He snorted. "Stop arguing with me. It'll get you nowhere."

"You're bossy," she said, as he fell into step with her. "Do you boss them around this way?"

"Someone has to," he said, looking at her sideways. He pushed his glasses up his nose, his hair falling into his eyes. He swept it away with an impatient hand. They came to her gate, and she turned to face him.

"Thank you." She gave him a quick grin. "I would have made it on my own though."

"I'm sure you would." He lifted his head slightly, breathing out through his nose. He looked as if he was going to say something important, and Lily tilted her head, waiting. He breathed out again and smiled at her. "See you tomorrow morning, Lily May." He started walking back towards the green.

Lily opened the gate and went in, watching him the whole time. She stopped at her door, and rummaged through her bag for her key. She looked back up towards where he was walking. He was under one of the trees in the green watching her. She hesitated slightly, not sure if he was trying to hide himself from her, but he lifted a hand in a wave and turned to walk away.

He was an enigma. One moment she felt right at home with him—he was relaxed and friendly—then the next moment she felt as if she was a bug under a microscope and he was studying her. It was perplexing.

She went inside and shut the door behind her. There was a note in the letterbox, and she assumed it was from the man Jake had seen. She went through to the kitchen, dropping her bag on the table as she opened the note and read it.

"Lynda. Sorry to have missed you."

It must be someone her mother knew. She closed it and propped it on the table for her to see when she got in. She got a glass of water, sat at the kitchen table, and made a start on her homework.

Friendship

Matt lay on his back looking up at the ceiling, watching the shadows dancing over the beams high above his head. Nate had lit the candles to give them some light. A fire in the middle of the room took the cold dampness from the air. The fire was smokeless, the flames a brilliant blue and red that told of it being magical and not physical. They were in the disused mill that sat beside the river that ran through Crowder Manor grounds. It was one of their favourite spots to meet. The waterwheel still turned outside, but the gears had been disconnected when the mill stopped grinding wheat into flour over fifty years ago.

"We like her," Josh said, throwing and catching a tennis ball in his hand. "We don't think she's dangerous. She needs us."

Jake was sitting crossed legged beside him, chewing on the side of his thumb nail. He lowered it long enough to agree with his brother. "She's pretty lost. You can see it in her eyes. She thinks she's got it together, thinks she's fine with moving, but she's not really. She needs friends; she just doesn't know it. Everyone needs friends."

"She's exhibited no signs of being like us." Nate pushed his glasses up his nose. "And she's given no signs that she knows what we are either. I didn't get any vibes from her, and she's pretty easy to read. I think it's pure chance she fitted yesterday. Matt, maybe you just felt a connection because, instinctively, you knew something was wrong with her and you tried to heal it subconsciously."

Matt blew out his breath and shrugged against the wooden floor. "Maybe. And your name?"

"I must had heard someone else say something that sounded like it." He shrugged. "I don't think we need to worry about her anymore."

"What? You want us to drop her? Fuck you!" Josh snapped. He glared at Nate where he leaned against the wall, one leg propped up.

"No, of course not! I merely meant we can be friends with her, get to know her better, and not worry about whether she's going to cause us trouble."

"Oh, I have a feeling she's going to cause us trouble," Matt murmured, still watching the shadows above his head. "She's cute, and I'd date her in a heartbeat. So would Josh and Jake, wouldn't you?"

"Too bloody right," Jake sniggered. "She caught our attention the moment she stepped into the classroom. So uptight in her shirt that's buttoned right up to her neck with her tie properly tied."

"And her skirt that hits just above her knees," Josh said, and threw Jake the ball. "And did you see those black knee highs socks and chunky shoes? She stands out without even trying, not to mention she's smart and easy to be around."

Jake sniggered and tossed the ball towards Matt, who lifted his hand and caught it without even looking.

"She was quick in French, fluent with only a couple of mistakes," Nate murmured and caught the ball that was thrown at him. "Intelligent and beautiful."

"She got a hundred percent on O'Connor's test. We thought he was going to ask her to marry him, he was so damn excited," Josh said and lifted his hand to Nate. Nate threw him the ball, and he tossed it to Matt, who had sat up.

"We were close to asking her," Jake snorted. "A hundred percent! She loves Maths, ergo she's perfect."

"So who gets to ask her out?" Matt asked, tossing the ball to Nate again.

"Well, we're not stepping back for you two." Josh snorted.

"You can't both date her at the same time," Matt exclaimed.

"Why not?" Josh demanded. "We'd treat her right."

"I know you would, but could you honestly see her letting you both date her? How would you manage dates to the cinema and stuff?"

"We'd take it in turns if she didn't want both of us with her," Jake answered.

"People don't do that! It'd be weird, and she'd never go for it," Nate snorted and tossed the ball at Josh a little harder. "And what makes you think she'd say yes to you two, and not me or Matt?"

Josh just grunted in reply and threw the ball to Jake.

"So what do we do? Toss a coin?" Matt asked in exasperation, catching the ball Jake tossed at him.

"Why don't we wait and let her choose?" Nate suggested. "We all like her, we all fancy her. She may not feel the same about us, and then this whole conversation is a waste of time. She might just view us as friends."

Matt threw the ball to Jake and lay back down on his back, folding his hands on his stomach.

"So, let's just keep it to friendship and see how it goes," Nate added and crouched down, balancing himself with his fingertips on the floor. "We've only known her for a couple of days. We may end up viewing her like a sister."

Josh snorted heavily and looked over at Jake with a shake of his head before speaking up. "Nate, not sure what floats your boat, bro, but we can guarantee we wouldn't have these kinds of thoughts over a sister."

"That's because you let the wrong fucking heads do your thinking!" Nate snapped and rolled his eyes when all they did was hoot with laughter, bumping their fists together. "Jesus, guys. If she could see you now, she'd run for the hills."

"If she could see us now, she'd have one of her fits, and we'd be doing a lot of explaining," Matt said dryly, pointing at one of the candles that was hanging in mid-air, suspended on nothing.

"Which reminds me," Nate said and picked up his phone. "I've researched this. If we're going to be spending time with her, and I know I aim to spend as much time as I can with her, then we need to know this."

Josh and Jake groaned when Nate said research. Josh leant backwards until his head was on Jake's knee, looking up at him. "Brace yourself, Nate has been let loose on the internet again."

"Well, Matt, it looks like it's just you and me that will know how to deal with her if she fits."

Josh sat straight up and faced Nate. "Go on, we're all ears."

"You're all bloody morons. Now pay attention. If she fits, she's going to fall, because for her it looks like her muscles go rigid in a seizure. If we can catch her, great, if not we have to make sure we clear the space around her so she can't hurt herself on anything. We need to time the seizure, that's the part where she's rigid, if it goes over five minutes we must phone for an ambulance. Once she starts to jerk and shake she's okay. We just make sure she doesn't get hurt then, and keep reassuring her that we're there."

"Don't we have to put something in her mouth to stop her from biting her tongue?" Jake asked.

"No, she could choke." Nate shook his head. "We really just have to let her go. Once she stops jerking we roll her onto her side and stay with her till she's with it completely, which can take a while, thirty minutes or longer."

"How long did it take her to come out of it?" Jake asked, sitting up to look at Nate.

"Well, she seemed fairly lucid quite quickly. She tried to get me to put her down. She knew what had happened. I didn't see her again after we left, though."

"O'Connor has us sitting on either side of her in Maths," Josh spoke up. "If she goes down on the steps we can catch her."

"We'll stick close in case she needs our help. I've also researched triggers, or potential triggers," Nate said. "She said she doesn't have photosensitive epilepsy, so flashing lights should be okay. But I suggest we keep close to her if we go anywhere like that with her. Tiredness, stress, and alcohol are all triggers—"

"Well, that rules out getting her drunk on her birthday." Jake let his breath out on a sigh.

"We aren't getting her drunk. Ever! You fucking reprobate," Josh snapped and smacked him up the back of the head.

"I'm getting drunk on my birthday. It's a rite of passage," Jake mumbled, rubbing the back of his head and glaring at Josh.

"Don't be an ass, we are not getting drunk on our birthday!"

"There doesn't have to be a 'we' in this, Joshua," Jake sneered.

"There's always a 'we', Jacob!" Josh snarled at his twin.

"Stop!" Matt got up onto his knees. "I am way too tired to deal with any cuts and bruises you two put on each other. No one is getting drunk on anyone's birthday. Imagine the chaos if we got out of control because we were drunk. We can't lose control like that, ever!"

"Jonas would skin you alive, right after I'd kicked you into next week!" Nate snapped.

"Fine," Jake grumbled, folding his arms. "I just wanted to get drunk once, that was all."

"Why?" asked Matt in surprise. He rarely heard the word I out of either of their mouths; it was always we. This was obviously something Jake was serious about.

"Just to see what it's like," he replied, with a shrug.

"Alright, alright," Nate said, holding up his hands. "After we're all eighteen, we'll get together here and you can get drunk to see what it's like. But just once and just us here!"

"Don't look at me when you have a hangover and can't think through a fucking migraine." Josh snorted.

"I won't look at you. I may be sick over you, though." Jake chuckled and avoided the head slap that was sent his way.

"If you're sick over me, I'll make you wash my clothes by hand!" Josh snapped and then ruined it by laughing. "Idiot."

"Moron."

"Okay, okay, you two can make up later." Matt stood up. "I'm going to bed or I'll never get up in time to pick Lily up. You wanna crash with me or go home?" he asked them.

"Crash with you." Nate looked at his watch. "It's well into the witching hours now."

"Frightened you'll get turned into a toad?" Josh chuckled, standing up and holding his hand out to Jake to help him up.

"No, but I may not make it to the end of the drive before I pass out."

They made their way outside. It was pitch black; the moon was almost new and there was no light. An owl hooted and its mate returned the call.

Flashlights were switched on and Nate snapped his fingers, extinguishing the flames in the upper room. The candles fell to the floor, making a thumping noise as they hit the wood. They would stay there until they needed them again.

"We'll have to bring Lily here," Matt said as they reached the edge of the woods. The manor ahead of them was dark. There were no lights on in the windows, and Matt knew his parents would be fast asleep now.

"Yeah, during the day, though," Josh said as they crossed the perfectly mowed lawns. Another owl hooted, but there was no reply this time. They rounded the house and let themselves in through the back door into the boot room. Silently, they crept through the house till they were in Matt's room. They'd done this hundreds of times over the years. None of their parents were surprised to find in the morning that they were all together, and they never bothered trying to stop it. The four of them had been a unit for as long as any of them could remember, and when they'd reached six and started to develop abilities that were different, they each turned to the other, rather than their parents. They'd instinctively known that if any of their parents found out it would cause trouble, so they were careful to keep it hidden from everyone but each other. Until Jonas.

Nate's was the only place they didn't camp down in and that was only because his room was too small. Matt's room was the usual go to place, though. The manor had spacious, high ceilinged rooms with large sash windows. Matt's room was no different, and with the bathroom opposite it was the best room for them all to stay together. They were here so often that they each had a change of clothes and nightwear in Matt's wardrobe.

Josh and Jake dragged out the spare double mattress that Matt kept under his bed and put the sheet over the top that their Aunt June demanded they use when they slept over. They'd have been happy just plopping down fully dressed and sleeping till morning, but Aunt June would have their hides if they did that. Nate and Matt shared the double bed and had done so since their first sleepover at five years old. Matt slept better when they were all in the room, but he never told them.

Once they were all settled, Matt switched off the overhead light and got into bed. Josh and Jake were on the mattress and already half asleep.

"See you in the morning," Matt spoke up and was rewarded with grunts from the twins. Nate muttered a good night, and it went quiet, save for the snores coming from the foot of the bed.

Moving Again

Lily finished the last piece of toast, her eyes on where her mother was cleaning the top of the counter with a cloth. She'd been scrubbing at the same spot for the past five minutes, and Lily didn't think it was because it was dirty.

"What's up?" she asked her quietly.

"Up? Nothing's up, Lily." Her mother's voice was bright. She gave the spot one last swipe and turned to face her, but her smile was strained and her eyes were darting around the room.

"Did you stain the counter?" Lily nodded to the counter. She crossed to the Bristol sink that sat under the mullioned window and washed up her plate.

"No, no. I just needed to clean up."

"The same spot for five minutes?"

"I hardly think so, dear," she replied, but it was vague. "Listen, darling, there's something I've been thinking about."

Lily watched her mother cross to sit at the table, the cloth still in her hands.

"What?"

"I'm not sure here is the best place for us right now. How about we find somewhere else? I was thinking Ireland. We've never been there."

"Ireland?" Lily gaped at her mother, not sure she was hearing her right.

"Yes, dear, I hear parts of it are beautiful, just waiting to be painted."

"Mum, you're under contract here. You signed for a year, they gave you a deposit. You said this was perfect. You were looking forward to the challenge of getting the four seasons in one place."

"I know, but well, things change. I changed. I don't think I'm feeling it." Her mother avoided her eyes in favour of a spot on the table that she began to scrub vigorously.

"Mum! You can't just up and leave, they won't understand. Hell, I don't understand." Lily was flustered, panic was edging into her mind. She couldn't face moving again. "It's my final year, Mum. I need these A levels if I want to go to a good Uni somewhere."

"I know, Lily, but you've always managed to settle quickly. It's still only your first week. You'd fit in somewhere else. You always do."

The world tipped beneath Lily's feet. Her hands gripped the edge of the china sink, trying to anchor herself against the rising panic inside her. She didn't want to leave here. She liked it here, she liked the quaint little cottage with its thatched roof and leaded windows. She liked the beams that ran across her bedroom ceiling. She liked her college, the teachers, and she liked the new friends she'd made. The boys. She liked the boys. She didn't want to say goodbye to it, to them. Not this quickly anyway.

"Lily, I just think we ought to move on."

"Mum, please. Listen to me. Every time you've wanted to move I've never made a fuss, have I? Not even this summer when we moved twice in four weeks! Please, Mum, I don't want to leave here. Not yet. I'm making friends here, Mum. Real friends." Desperation crashed through her.

"You've always enjoyed moving." Her mother got up and crossed back to the side. "Besides, you make friends wherever we go."

"Not this fast, usually it takes me until after Christmas before I'm fully accepted. But this time? I've made friends straight away. They're even going to celebrate my eighteenth with me, Mum. I've never had that before. I've never had friends with me on my birthday."

Her mother made a noise in the back of her throat. She pushed her hand onto her forehead as her eyes closed. "Lily, Lily, I'm sorry. I'm so sorry," she whispered. "It's been harder on you than I realised."

"Mum, please…"

There was a knock at the front door, and Lily looked at the clock on the wall. It was gone eight, and she'd missed her lift. Desperation turned to defeat. Her shoulders slumped. "I'll go. It's probably the post."

"No! Wait!" Her mother called out, but Lily was already in the hallway. She opened the cottage door and gave a gasp when she saw the twins standing on either side of the door, leaning on the door frame.

"You're late, Lily Pad—hey, what's wrong?"

"I'm… I'm sorry." She shook her head, her thoughts and emotions all over the place. "Let me get my bag. Sorry." She turned to see her mother standing in the doorway, her bag in her hands and regret on her face.

"Lily, we'll talk tonight," she said as Lily took the bag from her. "Who are your friends?"

Lily closed her eyes and shook her head before looking at her mother. "It won't matter who they are," she whispered. She reached forward and kissed her mother's cheek before going back to where the twins were still waiting for her.

Lily moved past them and shut the door behind her. She looked up, seeing the others waiting in the Land Rover.

"Oversleep?" Matt chuckled as she climbed into the front, putting her bag on the floor at her feet. She heard the twins get in on either side of Nate behind her. She shrugged, trying to swallow the lump that had settled in her throat. A feeling of overwhelming sadness was tugging at her. When her mother said they were moving, they moved. It was as simple as that.

She wasn't lying when she said she'd never made a fuss, she'd never felt connected with anywhere enough to want to stay. But it was different here, and she realised with a sinking feeling that it was the boys that made the difference. Two days in, and she was sucked in by them.

Two days.

She had to remind herself it was only two days. She didn't even know them that well. They were kind, good looking, and willing to be her friend. She had never needed friends before. Had never needed the connection that she knew they had. She was always content to drift along, having acquaintances that she could wave goodbye to at the end of the year and not shed a tear. So what made them different?

Nothing.

She was just being silly. They would lose no sleep if she left tomorrow and neither should she. She needed to keep telling herself that.

"Lily?" She felt her shoulder being nudged, and she blinked. She'd been lost in her own thoughts, but Nate snapped her out of it.

"Sorry, I was miles away, what did you say?" She pushed all her emotions down and turned to him.

"I was asking if you wanted to come out with us to Matt's house after college. Figured you'd like to see the house your mum is going to be painting.

"Dad won't be there, but Mum will be," Matt added. "She was raving this morning about the sketches your mum has already done."

Lily turned to look out of her window again, biting her lip. She didn't know what to do. If her mother suddenly decided to move to Ireland, she would be letting Matt's parents down. Her mother would pay back the down payment, she knew that, but it would be such a disappointment for them. And professionally, it wouldn't be good for her reputation. Her mother wouldn't worry about that, though. She sold every painting she did. An art gallery in London took them and none had ever come back. She worked in oils and the prices on some of the pictures had taken Lily's breath away, but she knew that there were a few collectors who bought a lot of her work. Some were even anxiously waiting for her next finished work.

"Lily Flower." Lily felt her shoulder being shaken again, and she realised that they were at college, parked in the same spot as yesterday. She reached down for her bag, and felt a hand on her back.

"You don't have to come over if you don't want to," Matt said quietly. "We won't hurt you, Lily. We just want to be your friends."

Lily felt the tears sting her eyes, and she turned her head away quickly, ashamed to cry in front of them. She couldn't say anything yet, not to Matt at least. He was their son, and if her mother did decide to throw the job in, she wouldn't want them finding out from him.

"I'd love to, but I don't think I can make it tonight." Her voice was thick with unshed tears. She couldn't look at him as she got out. If they were moving, there really was no point in Lily making this harder than it was. And going by experience, when she got home she'd be helping to pack up again.

"Okay, no worries," Matt said gently. "Maybe next time."

Lily bit her lip and nodded jerkily. "I need to use the loo," she said, keeping her head turned away. "I'll see you all later. Thanks for the ride." She turned and made a dash for the front entrance and the safety of the girls' toilets.

There were a few girls in there, too busy applying makeup and chatting with their friends to notice her. She locked herself into a cubicle and sat on the seat, hugging her bag to her chest. Tears came to her eyes, and she let them slide down her face. She'd never cried at leaving before. She'd never regretted leaving anywhere enough to cry. She was used to coming home on the last day of school to find her mother already talking about where she had decided to move. But she'd never said goodbye to real friends before.

Two days.

She had to remember it was only two days. She didn't know them that well. So why did it feel as if her heart was being dragged from her chest?

She didn't know anything about them. She didn't know what they liked, or didn't like, to eat. She didn't know what their favourite colour was, or what music they listened to. She didn't know any of a hundred things people knew about their friends.

But she did know that they were kind. That Nate had picked up her when she needed it most. She knew that when he held her she felt safe for the first time during a seizure. She knew that Matt was a gentle flirt and that he liked peas. She knew that Josh and Jake were the jokers of the pack, but inseparable. She knew Nate was the leader of their group and that what he said went. She knew that he was curious about her, but he still accepted her. They wanted to be her friends, were going to celebrate her birthday with her.

No one had ever done that before.

They'd given her nicknames. Silly, stupid nicknames that made her feel warm inside.

No one had ever done that before either.

The overhead bell rang, and Lily jumped. She was going to be late. She left the cubicle to find the room was empty. She caught sight of her reflection in the mirror and grimaced. Her eyes were puffy from crying and the end of her nose was red. She quickly rinsed her face with cold water and dried it on a paper towel, but she still looked like she'd been crying. The overhead bell ringing again told her she'd missed registration. She closed her eyes and counted to ten. If she moved away from here, missing registration wasn't really going to matter.

She left the toilets and headed towards the Maths department. She was going to be late if she didn't get a move on, but it was as if she had lead weights in her shoes. She finally made it to class and when she opened the door, Mr O'Connor was in full swing. Now she was going to have to get to her seat, knowing that everyone would see her face and know she'd been crying. Not to mention she was going to be in trouble with him.

"Sorry I'm late, sir. I was—" she started to speak to Mr O'Connor as she crept towards the steps that led to her seat but he cut her off.

"Ah, Miss Adair, sit yourself down. Nethercott informed me you weren't feeling too sharp this morning. We're going through page forty-five when you get settled." He turned back to the board.

She got to her seat, keeping her head down and avoiding eye contact with anyone. She drew her books from her bag, found the correct page, and shut out anything except Mr O'Connor's voice. She didn't dare look at either of the twins.

By the time the bell rang for the end of class, she had a headache behind her eyes that was making her feel sick. All she needed now was to flip and have a seizure. She drew in a deep breath as she shoved her books into her bags.

"Thanks for covering for me with him," she said, aware that they were still sitting in their seats.

"No worries, we covered you with Peters as well. Told him you had a headache."

"Thank you," she said and got up. They both stood at the same time and waited for her to move.

She bit her lip, shouldered her bag and started down the steps. She knew they were behind her, but they said nothing, and she didn't know what else to say, either. She had to get it together though or spend the day in floods of tears.

She forced herself to smile as she turned to them outside the classroom. "See you later, and thanks again for covering for me."

"Lily." Josh stepped forward, his hand on the strap of his bag. "Are you okay?"

"I'm fine. Just a headache," she said. "I'll see you."

She hurried off in the direction of her French class, just making it before she was late again. She settled into her seat, sending Nate a watery smile. She just hoped that she didn't still look as if she'd cried. Nate made no mention of her running off that morning and started up a conversation on the homework they'd had the day before. She found herself relaxing, and her headache receded as she talked to him.

"Today, you're going to pair off into couples and discuss any subject from the list on the board. French only, no English." Madam Fontaine started the class the way she meant it to carry on: in French.

Lily saw a few people get up and swap out chairs as they chose who they wanted to partner up with. Lily looked at Nate out of the corner of her eye and wondered if he'd choose someone else. But he was intent on the board, the overhead light reflecting on his glasses so she couldn't see his eyes. He was wearing a black sweater over his white shirt today, and she could just see his tie at the collar of his shirt. His hands were clasped on the desk in front of him, a muscle worked along his jawline. His dark hair was pushed back from his forehead, but she knew it would soon flop forward when he ran a hand through it.

"Education?" Nate asked in French.

"What?" Lily was thrown, not expecting him to stay with her.

"I suggest we discuss education, unless you'd prefer something else?" He turned his head slightly, his eyes focused on her.

Lily looked up at the board, more to get her thoughts under control than to see what else was up there. "Okay, that's fine," she said.

"French, Mademoiselle Adair," Madam Fontaine called out, and Lily flushed.

"Tell me about your last school, Lily May." Nate's French was flawless.

"There's not much to tell," she replied. *"It was bigger than this one, more students. About a thousand more. What's your favourite subject?"*

"Biology. I want to be a dentist."

Lily's eyes went wide, and she covered her mouth with her hand to stop a giggle escaping. "Really?"

"French," he reminded her in a whisper. *"Yes, really. Is that so hard to believe?"* he added, a touch of defensiveness in his voice.

"No, of course not, just unexpected," she replied with a shrug. *"What subjects do you need for that?"*

"I need A's in Chemistry, Biology, Physics and Maths. I'm studying them all here, so I hope to get into Uni next September."

"Maths? You aren't in our maths class though."

"My physics class is then. I have Maths when you take Geography and the others are in Latin. I was fortunate that

O'Connor let me sit in on his Year 12 classes and sets me different work."

"Couldn't you drop French and take Maths then?"

"I want to keep a language," he murmured, pushing his glasses up his nose. Lily was beginning to get an idea of just how smart he was if Mr O'Connor was willing to make a placement for him to get A level maths.

"I'm impressed," she told him, smiling at him. His eyes dropped to her cheek, and she frowned. Did she have something on there? She lifted a finger to her face, but he caught her hand in his and smoothed his thumb over her cheek.

"You have cute dimples when you smile," he whispered. He stroked his finger gently over her cheek. But she wasn't smiling now. His thumb was soft on her skin, a tiny caress that made her breath catch and her heart flip.

"I know French is the language of love, Monsieur Cohen, but perhaps we can keep to the subjects on the board, no?"

Nate shifted, dropped her fingers and pushed his glasses up his nose. Lily coloured up as Madame Fontaine patted Nate on the shoulder and carried on walking around the students. She looked back up at the board in an attempt to erase the feeling of his finger from her cheek.

"What do you want to do when you leave?" Nate spoke up, and she looked back at him.

"I have no idea," she admitted. *"I suppose try to get into a Uni somewhere, but I don't know what I want to do ultimately."*

"Your French is very good," Nate pointed out. *"What else are you taking?"*

"History, Geography, Maths, English Literature, and Language."

"Have you thought of anything at all?" He tilted his head to one side. His expression was open, and Lily felt relaxed again.

"It's all up in the air. Uni means staying in one place for three years, and I don't know if my mum can do that."

The words were out before she'd even realised she was thinking them, and they came out in English. She looked around quickly, but Madame Fontaine was on the other side of the classroom. Her eyes caught the girl who had spoken to Nate yesterday. She couldn't remember her name, but she was watching Lily, and the look on her face wasn't pleasant. Lily rolled her eyes and looked back at Nate; she couldn't be bothered with catfights over boys. In her experience, boys weren't worth that kind of effort. She caught Nate's eyes. He was watching her closely, concern on his face.

Maybe there were some boys worth the effort.

"Lily, if you want to go to University, go for it," he said quietly. *"You can get a shared room with other students. You don't have to stay with your mum forever. It's your life, Lily May. Live it."*

She smiled sadly, looking down at his clasped hands on the table. *"I want to be independent, but there are certain things I can't do. I can't take a bath unless someone is in the house with me. I can't drive, I can't be left alone in a kitchen. I nearly set our house on fire once. I was fourteen and we were in London. Mum was at the gallery, and I was home alone. We had a gas fire in the living room. I went in there to do my homework. I had a seizure and knocked everything off the coffee table. My homework got knocked into the fire and caught the rug on fire."*

He slid his hands forward and gripped hers as she spoke. She looked up at him, putting a bright smile on her face. *"It was okay. The fire alarms went off, and our neighbour called the fire brigade when they didn't stop. They contained the fire to the room, and I was fine. We moved the next week."*

"Shit, Lily May, that's not okay," he murmured. "You could have been killed."

"But I wasn't." She shrugged. *"We learnt our lesson. I'm not left alone, and if for any reason I am alone, I don't go anywhere near fires."* She tried to make a joke of it, but he didn't laugh. He just gripped her hands tightly, his intense eyes watching her closely.

"Have you ever hurt yourself during a fit?"

"No more than the next person with epilepsy," she shrugged, uncomfortable with talking about it. *"Is that a 'show me your scars and I'll show you mine' offer, Jonathan?"* she joked. He dropped his head and looked at her over the top of his glasses, one eyebrow rose and a smirk tugged one side of his lips upwards. Lily's insides squeezed together, he was wickedly gorgeous when he did that.

"I like that idea, Lily May," he murmured. *"But it's not Jonathan either."*

"Will you ever tell me?" she asked, unable to keep the smile from her lips.

"I might."

He held her eyes, his thumbs moving slowly in a gentle circle on the back of her hands.

Madame Fontaine clapped her hands together to get everyone's attention. Nate let go of her hands, and they turned in their seats to face the front again. Lily missed his touch.

"Homework for tomorrow. Write up your conversations with each other today. Keep your verbs tight."

The overhead bell rang, and Lily stretched in her seat. Her headache had receded, and she felt content as she looked over at Nate.

"You sure you don't want to come over tonight? We can do the homework together," he said, picking up his bag and slinging the handle over his head.

She'd forgotten about it. In her conversation with him, she'd completely forgotten what her mother had said to her that morning. A black cloud descended over her head, and it wiped the smile from her face. She sat forward and picked up her bag.

"Nate, I'm not sure—" She started to tell him what her mother had said and then remembered that his family was Matt. She couldn't ask him to keep it quiet from Matt. She didn't have that right.

"Don't worry, Lily. You've only just moved in. You're probably still trying to get straight."

That wasn't the problem though, the problem was that instead of unpacking, she could well be packing.

Holding Hands

When Matt dropped her off outside her gate, she was exhausted. She'd tried hard to keep it down all day by refusing to think about it. She was good at burying her head in the sand, so she'd spent the rest of the day keeping her mind as far from thoughts of moving as she could. With each lesson, she'd pushed herself to concentrate harder. It was easy to throw herself into her studies and shut the rest of the world out.

Lunchtime found her once again sitting with them at their table in the canteen. The twins had mucked about the whole time, keeping Lily laughing at their antics until her face hurt.

The car ride home was just as loud, with Josh and Jake messing about until Nate threatened to make them walk. Matt stopped, and Nate swapped seats with Josh, so that he was on the side and Josh was in the middle. Lily noticed that they seemed to calm down when they were beside each other. She also noticed how at any given time they seemed to be touching each other. Whether it was an arm around a neck or just sitting pressed against each other, there was contact between them of some sort.

"Hey, Lily Flower," Matt called out of his window as she started to open her gate. She looked back at him. "See you tomorrow," he called.

She made no reply, not sure what she could say to that. It all depended on what would be said once she got behind her front door. She lifted her hand in reply and smiled at them before going inside. She let her bag drop to the floor at her feet.

"Mum? I'm home."

She heard a noise in the kitchen and went through, leaving her bag behind. Her mother was sitting at the table, a piece of paper in her hands. She looked up and Lily could see the lines of strain in her face before she smoothed them away with a smile.

"Lily, did you have a good day?" she asked.

Lily slumped into the chair opposite her. "It was okay. Mum, about this morning."

Her mother folded the paper and got up, putting it into the letter rack that stood on the shelf by the back door. "I was hasty this morning. I didn't really explain things properly to you."

Lily sat up straighter. "What do you mean?"

"It was just an idea, not a hard and fast plan." Her mother kept her back to her as she moved across to the sink. "I keep moving you around, and you've never complained. I've stolen your childhood from you, and I'm so sorry."

Lily processed her words and the regret behind them; she jumped to her feet and crossed to her. "Mum, you've stolen nothing from me."

"But I have." Her mother turned and Lily saw the unshed tears in her eyes. "You've never had proper friends. You've never had sleepovers, a BFF, or whatever they're calling best friends these days. You've never had a birthday party, had all your friends over…" she faded out sadly.

"I've never wanted that. I can honestly say, hand on my heart, that I have never once regretted how we've lived. I didn't miss anything, Mum."

"Until now. Something's happened, or you've met someone, and you've realised what you've never had."

"No, it's not like that." Lily flapped her hands slightly and then bit her lip. "I have met someone; I've met some people that I really like. They've accepted me into their group, they've made me feel welcome, and I like it. Matt…" She faded out, guilt wormed its way in over making her mother sad.

"You keep mentioning him." Her mother smiled. "I'll take care of things, I promise. It'll be fine. You're not a child anymore, and I have to remember that."

Lily blushed as she realised her mother thought she liked Matt as more than a friend. Truth be told she liked them all a little too much, but something she said caught at her.

"What do you mean take care of things?"

"What? Oh, I just mean I'll go off for a day trip somewhere and paint what I see. I don't have to contain myself to just painting the manor. The sea isn't far; I can paint some seascapes."

Something about her mother's bright words didn't ring true, but Lily didn't push it. She was too excited with the possibility that she could stay.

"So, we're staying then?" she asked tentatively. She held her breath and watched as her mother turned from the sink and pulled her into a hug that Lily returned easily.

"Yes, dear, we're staying here for as long we can."

Lily squealed and kissed her mother's cheek noisily. "Thank you! Thank you!"

"Don't deafen me." Her mother laughed, but it was still strained, and when Lily pulled back to look at her, there were tears in her eyes again. The guilt returned stronger.

"Mum, do you really need to go?" she asked quietly.

"No, I don't. I want you to have a fantastic year. I want you to do all the things you want to do. I want you to make friends and be free, Lily. I just want you to be happy."

"I am happy."

"Good. No more now, it was a moment of madness. I'll fix us something to eat and then we can sit down and watch a film together. I feel as if we haven't spent any time together for ages."

Lily grinned at her mother and hugged her again. "I'll get my homework done quickly."

She went back to get her bag. Her heart was feeling much lighter now that she knew she was staying. But there was a tiny niggling doubt that her mother was only doing it for her.

Lily woke up suddenly from a deep sleep. There was someone in her room.

Fear held her tightly, her heart beating, eyes wide against the darkness of the night. She gripped the blankets in her hands and held her breath, her ears strained to listen carefully. Silence was the only thing she heard and there was no movement. She moved her hand carefully until she could feel the switch on her bedside lamp. She flicked it on and sat up, her heart thumping as she looked around her room. Her empty room.

She let her breath out on a whoosh. She must have dreamt it. Her heart was still beating madly as she looked towards her window. Her curtains were open, but she couldn't see out with the light on. She looked around her small room once more and then switched off the light. Slipping from the bed, she crossed to the window seat to look for stars. The angle was awkward, so she slid the sash window up and leant forward. The scent of the trees and the distant smell of the sea drifted on the breeze and she inhaled deeply, her eyes closing as she leant on her arms.

"*Lilith.*"

She almost fell forward out of her window, her eyes flying open. It was a whisper on the breeze, coming from outside not behind her. She pulled back into the safety of her room, her hands on the sash, ready to slam it down. She searched the dark shadows of the garden, but she couldn't see anyone. Her eyes went to the tree line, seeing nothing except the dark shapes of the bushes and trees. Sighing heavily, she shook her head. She wasn't usually fanciful. Maybe the stress of the last couple of weeks was playing with her head. She slid the window down, leaving it open a few inches, and got back into bed. There was no one there, and no one had called her name.

When her alarm woke her, she felt heavy headed, as if she hadn't slept very well at all. Her dreams were an odd collection of things; something to do with her mother, but when she tried to capture any of it they drifted away like cobwebs on the breeze.

Breakfast was coffee, toast, and a quick look through the newspapers. It was one of the first things her mother did wherever they went, sometimes even before she connected the electric. She would find the nearest newsagents and put in for three newspapers to be delivered daily. The national newspaper, the local newspaper to the area, and one of what her mother called the gutter newspapers. Lily had asked why she had the gutter newspaper if she thought it was trash. Her reply was that they tended to report on things that were ridiculous but sometimes the ridiculous was true. The answer had confused her then, and it still did now. She hurriedly turned the page, quickly hiding the image of a scantily dressed female displaying her breasts for all the readers to see.

"Lily, I want to get some pictures of the manor in the twilight. Mr Crowder has said I can go along this evening. He's invited us to dinner with them. I think you may have met Matt anyway, haven't you?" she asked casually, but the smile on her lips told Lily she was teasing.

"I may have done," she said, refusing to bite. She looked back down at the story of a woman who claimed her dog was taken by aliens for experimentation and then returned as a cat. Did people believe this stuff?

"Good, we're to get there for six. I got the impression dinner will be a semi-formal affair."

"I have to wear a tux?" Lily inquired, sending her mother a wink.

"Yes, and spats," her mother replied. Lily laughed and checked her watch; she had to make a move or be late again. She got up, taking her dishes to the sink, and then grabbed her bag. She dropped a kiss on her mother's head and headed towards the front door.

"Take your coat. It's supposed to rain later!" her mother called. Lily grabbed her jacket from the peg and stuffed her feet into her shoes. They were nicely broken in, and she didn't need to undo the laces anymore.

"See you, Mum." She called out her goodbye and headed out of the door, banging it shut behind her as she slung her bag over her shoulder. There was no sign of the others yet, but she was a few minutes early. She didn't want them to have to call for her again, or worse, leave without her because she was unreliable.

She sat on the wall that edged the front garden and looked up and down the road. Three identical cottages stood opposite hers, and that was the sum total of Derry's Lane. Looking left she could see the road was lined with hedges and trees, some of them just starting to turn in colour with the approach of autumn. The national speed limit signs, set just after the last cottage, showed it was the edge of the village. She looked down the other way towards the green and sighed. It was beautiful here. Small, but beautiful. There was a stillness here that settled her deep inside.

She heard a car and turned her head thinking it was Matt, but it was a dark car coming down the road. As it neared, it slowed right down until it was level with her. The front windows were tinted and it wasn't until it slid down that she could see anyone inside. A man sat in the driver's seat, a smile on his handsome face.

"Hey, can you tell me where I can find Mrs Johnston's place?" His smile revealed a crooked eye tooth. His dark eyes seemed like liquid as he watched her. He was handsome, and she found herself smiling back at him.

"I'm sorry, I just moved here. I don't know where anyone lives yet." She heard another car and saw Matt's Land Rover coming up. "Matt might, he lives here," she told him, pointing at the Land Rover. She jumped down from the wall as Matt slowed, his window opening.

"Everything alright?" he called out, a deep frown between his eyes.

"Where's Mrs Johnston live?"

"Number four, Toll Lane. Second road around to the left."

Lily repeated it to the man in the car, and he grinned at her.

"Thanks. That's the good thing about small communities, everyone knows everyone. See you around, beautiful." He winked at her, his smile becoming slightly sardonic. She had the feeling he despised small village life or he was laughing at some joke she didn't know. He drove forward, and she watched as the car disappeared around the end of the road.

"Hey, Lily Pad, c'mon. Another day of institutionalized learning awaits us." She went over and climbed into the passenger seat.

"Who was that?" Matt asked, and she shrugged.

"No idea, never seen him before." She looked behind her at the others. "Hey, guys."

"Good morning, Lily May," Nate said softly. He wasn't wearing glasses today, and Lily did a double take. He was hot with glasses, without he was breath-taking. His crystal blue eyes were clear to see, and it made his cheekbones stand out even more.

"What happened to your glasses?"

"Matthew happened," he said and let out a long sigh. Lily grinned, looking over at Matt.

"What did you do?"

"He sat on them," Josh answered for him.

"And broke the frame," Jake finished, and then they both started to laugh.

"It's not funny!" Nate whined. "I'm practically blind without them!"

"You have contacts in; you're hardly blind, Nate. And I already told you I'd take you to the optician's after college to get them fixed," Matt said with a sigh.

"Oh, yeah," Josh sat forward now that he was in the middle. "Lily Pad, we'll be taking a detour after college."

"That's okay, I'll catch the bus." She almost felt him roll his eyes as he sighed heavily. He leant his chin on her shoulder.

"Nope." He popped the 'p'. "We"—his breath fanned over her ear, sending a shiver down her spine—"includes you now. You haven't seen the town yet, have you? We'll get Nate sorted with his glasses, and then we'll nip in for a pizza."

"Well, I don't know, my mum—"

"Text her." Matt cut her off gently.

"No. I mean, yes. I mean, she told me we were supposed to be at your house tonight," she spoke to Matt, hyper aware of how close Josh still was. If she moved at all, his nose would brush against her skin.

"Really? Nothing was said this morning to me. What's that for?"

"Mum wants some photos of the manor in twilight, and your dad invited us for dinner at six. Semi-formal affair apparently." She kept perfectly still.

"Oh, bloody hell." Nate grunted. "Alright, we'll postpone till tomorrow for my glasses."

"It's okay, I can go on the bus. You have to get your glasses fixed, Nate," she said. Josh shook his head, and she felt his nose brush her skin. It sent a frisson of sensation zinging through her. He moved back and relief was tinged with regret; a regret that she didn't quite understand, so she ignored it.

"I've got an idea," Jake spoke up. "We get out in time to nip down to the optician's today. We can drop Lil on the way back to change, and then we can go for pizza after college sometime next week."

"Good thinking, Jacob," Josh said, and held out his hand for Josh to shake.

"Why thank you, Joshua," he replied primly, accepting his hand and making Lily giggle. She looked at Matt. He was grinning as he steered the Land Rover through the winding lanes.

"All in favour?" Nate asked, and four ayes were heard. "I said all in favour? Do try to keep up, Lily May."

"Aye," she said quietly, and she felt fingers slide across the back of her neck quickly, but she wasn't sure who it was. "Do you always vote on things like that?" she asked.

"I guess." Josh spoke as if he'd not really thought about it. "I don't remember a time when we didn't vote on things. I know Nate likes to think he runs the show, but it's mostly just us letting him think that."

"I don't think it, Joshua, I know it.".

"Careful there, Nate," Josh said. "One could always let slip what Nate is short for. One doesn't think you've been brave enough to let Lily Pad know yet, have you?"

"It's nothing to do with bravery," Nate spluttered. "And if one doesn't shut up, one will be hurting."

Lily turned in her seat to look at Josh. "So what is Nate short for?"

"I'll tell her, not you!" Nate shoved Josh. "When I'm good and ready. Besides, I'm waiting to see if you can guess first, Lily May."

"Really?" Lily grinned at him. "And what do I get when I get it right?"

"Jesus, Lily, don't ask him that," Matt shot out, laughing.

"You get the dubious honour of being one of a very small number of people who know," Nate said, glaring at the back of Matt's head. His eyes slid to Lily's, and she saw a gleam of wickedness there. "Unless there's something else you would like from me?"

Lily blushed when she realised how her words could be taken. She turned around abruptly.

"Oh, look, cows." She pointed out of her window at a group of cows in the field they were passing. There was a snigger from the back and then a thump, but nothing could make her turn around now. Her face was far too red, especially since she'd just compounded her embarrassment by saying something as dumb as, *oh, look, cows!*

Trying to cover her embarrassment, she fished her phone out of her bag and sent her mum a quick text letting her know she'd be a bit later and why. Matt reached forward to put the stereo on, and music blasted out that had the twins singing along. She was glad of the diversion, but still couldn't look at any of them. The song changed, and she recognised it and began to sing along quietly. They all knew this one and belted it out loudly.

By the time they reached the college, Lily was happily singing along with them, her earlier embarrassment forgotten. Matt turned off the engine, and Lily moved to open her door.

"You're on your own for last class again." Matt put his hand on her shoulder to stop her getting out. "Don't hang around waiting for us. Come straight here, okay?"

"Okay, thanks." She nodded. He winked at her and squeezed her shoulder gently before letting go and jumping out his own side. She got out and shut her door, the twins came up to her.

"C'mon, Lily Pad, let's go get registered." Jake gripped her hand and started to pull her along.

"I can find my way now, Jake," she insisted. His hand was cool against her own, his fingers curled around hers tightly. She made no move to loosen his hold. Her heart skipped a beat and heat flooded her cheeks.

He looked at her sideways as they walked, a smirk played around his lips. "I'm Joshua," he said.

She narrowed her eyes at him, certain she had it right when she called him Jake. She studied his profile as they walked and then looked to see where Josh—Jake—was. He was coming up behind her, a matching smirk on his face. He caught up, took her bag and then caught her hand in his. She blinked, thrown from her thoughts of figuring out which was which. They were both holding her hands, and it made her feel… she wasn't sure how it made her feel. She'd held hands before, although granted, never two boys at a time. But it hadn't felt quite like this before; even though she wasn't quite sure how it felt yet. One thing she did know was that it wasn't a bad feeling.

At least it wasn't until she saw the looks they were getting from the people they were passing in the corridors. She pulled her hands free and stuck them into her jacket pockets, putting her head down. She could feel the heat in her cheeks.

"What's up? Are we contagious?"

"Everyone is staring," she told them.

"So? Who gives a fuck?"

"They're going to think—" She snapped her mouth shut. They were going to think she was dating both of them at the same time. And she wasn't even dating one of them.

"And in which realm would it matter what someone else thinks?" snorted Jake/Josh, she was almost certain it was Jake now. "I'm your friend, Jacob is your friend. Friends hold hands all the time. How many times have we watched you girls band together and hold hands going to the toilet?"

"So you hold Nate's hand as you walk into the loo?" she inquired, certain that she hadn't mixed them up.

"If he feels lonely." He shrugged casually and then ruined it by sniggering. They stopped outside the classroom.

"That I have to see," she said with a laugh. They leant against the wall, shoulders touching, and she took the opportunity to really study them as she stood in front of them. They watched her through strands of dark hair, their chins tilted down slightly, and their arms folded. They really were handsome, but she'd caught one of their tells. They'd been trying to catch her out, but there were small things that told them apart that she didn't think they were aware of, and she wasn't going to tell them. In this case, they crossed their arms differently, something she'd already seen.

She stepped closer to who she was now certain was Josh. She stood toe to toe with him, so close she could feel his breath fanning over her face. His lips twisted into a sinful smirk as he watched her through his fringe. She reached up, a grin on her lips as she kept eye contact with him. Slowly, she slid her hand into the inside of his jacket pocket, her fingers closed over the smooth, round tin of the button badge.

"Hello, Joshua," she whispered. She stepped back, and her hand slipped free of his jacket. She uncurled her fingers, and held out the button badge to him. She saw his smirk grow, and then he reached forward to take the badge from her. He let his fingertips trail over her palm, making her shiver at the contact, his eyes never leaving hers.

"Well done, Lilith." The shiver extended down her spine. She'd never heard her name purred quite like that.

"Okay, people." Mr Peters broke the moment as he came down the corridor with a stack of yet more papers. "You know the drill now. Sarah, get the door if you would."

Lily stepped back from the twins and took her bag. Jake caught her hand before she could move right away; he stepped forwards till his mouth was by her ear.

"What gave us away?" he whispered, and the shiver became a shudder. They were affecting her in ways she'd never experienced before.

"I'm not telling," she whispered back. She felt his lips brush her ear, and then he was moving back from her. Lily's breathing wasn't quite even as she went into the classroom. She saw them move ahead of her, shoulders bumping as they walked with their heads bent together. She took a deep breath and shook her head. She was attracted to them, and that was a perfectly normal reaction when faced with how gorgeous they were, but it didn't mean any of them were attracted to her, or that she should read into anything that wasn't there. They wanted to be friends with her, and that was all it was. She wasn't going to ruin that by being stupid.

Rain Check

They'd left the college grounds quickly after final bell. Matt managed to get out of the car park before the buses started to leave, so it hadn't taken them long to get into town and park up.

"Shame we can't grab a pizza," Jake murmured, rubbing his stomach as he jumped down from the Land Rover.

"You can," Nate spoke up. He pulled his tie off and undid his top button. "We'll wait for you if we get done first."

Lily closed her door and looked up and down the high street. From where she was standing, she could see a couple of second hand shops, a pet store, two cafes, and a clothing shop. She would like to come back another time and explore. Matt had found a spot just outside the optician's, and Lily was impressed by his skill in parallel parking.

"Ten minutes," Josh called, already crossing the street with Jake beside him.

"C'mon, Flower." Matt tapped her shoulder, ran his fingers down her arm and caught her hand in his. He led her to where Nate was holding the glass door open for her. She let him tug her inside but kept her eyes on Nate. She wondered what he thought about Matt holding her hand. He gave no reaction, just smirked at her as she passed him. He went over to the main desk, and they went across to the racks of men's glasses.

"Will they be able to fix them?" Lily asked as Matt let go of her hand to take a pair of black framed glasses.

"I think so." He slid them onto his nose. "Nethercotts! To which one am I speaking?" He did an excellent imitation of Mr O'Connor, making her laugh.

"Are you with Nate for Maths then?" she asked him, trying on different pairs of glasses and pulling faces at him. "You're not with us."

"No, I'm in O'Connor's Trig and Calc class." He moved over to the ladies' frames. He picked out a bright pink framed pair and put them on.

Lily laughed and reached up to touch the frames. "They suit you," she giggled. He caught her hand and tugged her slightly closer to him.

"What are you saying, Lily?" He arched an eyebrow at her, a tiny smirk tugging at the corner of his lips.

"Pink is your colour. It brings out the brown in your eyes." She grinned up at him.

"It brings out the weird in him." Nate joined them and reached out for a pair of black frames. He slid them onto Lily's face and smiled. "These suit you."

"Yeah, they do," Matt agreed, putting the pink ones back. "You look cute."

She caught Matt's eyes, and her smile faded. His whiskey eyes were intent on her face, and it made her toes curl.

"Did they fix them for you?" she asked Nate brightly, dragging her gaze to him and away from Matt.

"They're going to. I have to come back Monday for them," he said quietly.

Matt reached out and slid his fingers along the frames of the glasses, his fingertips trailed over her skin. He pushed his hands into her hair, unhooked the glasses and drew them slowly down, his fingers brushing against her skin. His eyes held hers, and she was completely unable to stop the shudder that overtook her. His eyes dropped to her lips as he slid the glasses free, and it made Lily's breath catch. Her whole world narrowed to just him.

"We can go now," Nate said softly.

Lily drew in a sharp breath, flustered at her reaction to him. This was ridiculous. She was feeling things for all of them that she had no right to be feeling. It was basic attraction, that much she understood. But to feel more than attraction would be bad, and to feel it for all of them would be a disaster.

She turned to leave, annoyed with herself. She rushed through the door and collided with what felt like a brick wall. Her face was shoved against a rough wool coat that smelt good. Hands gripped her shoulders, and she was held tightly, stopping her from falling.

"Whoa, where's the fire?"

She looked up and recognised the man she'd spoken to that morning in the car. He seemed to make the connection at the same time as recognition dawned on his face.

"Well, hello again, beautiful." He smiled widely at her. She felt her cheeks burn in embarrassment as she bit her lip.

"I am so sorry," she breathed out. "Did I hurt you?"

He laughed as if the idea of her hurting him was ludicrous.

"If I say yes, would it guilt you into going to get some coffee with me?" he asked her, his hands still on her shoulders. His eyes were a liquid black, but there was no emotion reflected in them, and it made her uneasy. His skin had a slightly olive tone to it, and his hair was black as ink, thick, wavy, and on the long side. Her first impression that he was attractive was spot on, but his eyes looked dead.

"We have to go now," Nate spoke up and his voice was icy cold. Lily frowned and looked around at him. He was right behind her, his arms folded as he stared at the stranger. Matt was right beside him with an identical stance. Lily had the vague idea that this must be like having older brothers. They were clearly not happy with the stranger and were showing it, but she had no idea why.

Her shoulders were released, and he moved past her into the optician's.

"I've rented the cottage opposite yours, beautiful. Maybe we can take a rain check on the coffee," he said as he passed her. He showed no reaction at all to the animosity rolling off the boys. He didn't even acknowledge their presence as he carried on into the opticians. Lily shrugged it off and looked back at Matt and Nate.

"C'mon, Lil," Matt said, and she went with them to the Land Rover. He unlocked the doors, and she climbed in.

Neither of them looked happy. She doubted it was the odd man that made them unhappy. She wondered if she'd done something wrong, if she was who they were unhappy with. Maybe Nate didn't like Matt touching her face like that. But he'd seen her hold hands with him and hadn't said anything. And if she was honest, Nate had made no real indication that he liked her like that anyway. Sure, he'd held her hands whilst she told him about her seizures, but that could have been nothing more than friendly concern. In fact, when she thought about it, none of them had made any indication that they were interested in anything but friendship. Not really.

She made an impatient sound in the back of her throat. She had to stop this. She had to stop thinking like this. She was going to let it ruin the friendship she was building with them. She wasn't in a position to have a serious relationship with anyone anyway; she had to remember that. Even if she was normal, and didn't have a seizure at the drop of a hat, she knew without a doubt that come the summer holidays she'd be moving, and most probably she would never see them again. Sadness slid through her.

"We got half and half," came a cheerful voice, breaking her from her thoughts. Matt and Nate were still outside the Land Rover, and she could see they were talking intently. Josh and Jake got into the Land Rover, the smell of pizza made her stomach rumble loudly and her mouth fill with saliva.

"Was that thunder?"

Lily blushed and rubbed her hand over her stomach. "Well, it wasn't me, so it must have been the roll of distant thunder," she said, making them laugh. Matt got into the front, and she heard Nate get into the back, slamming his door shut.

"We've got half Hawaiian, half Meat Feast on one." Josh spoke as soon as the door was shut.

"Three Cheeses and Veggie on the other."

"Meat feast, please," Matt said. "Six is still ages away, and they won't actually eat till closer to six thirty, Lily. Have a slice."

"Keep the thunder at bay." Josh sniggered and handed Matt a slice of pizza.

"Veggie, please," she said and turned to take the slice from Jake. It went silent as they ate the pizza. Lily picked off a piece of feta and popped it into her mouth, it was delicious.

"Lily, it's none of our business, but don't take that rain check." Nate's sudden words took her a moment to process.

"Well, that's a contradiction." Josh snorted. "And what are we talking about anyway?"

Lily kept quiet, using the pizza as an excuse not to speak. She wanted to know what they would say to the twins if she didn't say anything.

"Lily bumped into someone leaving the optician's," Matt spoke up. "I think it was the guy in the BMW this morning. He asked her to go for a coffee with him."

"What? Out of the blue?" Josh demanded.

"I expect he was just being nice about me trying to mow him over," Lily finally said, and took another bite.

"He was creepy," Nate corrected her. "He tried to guilt you into going with him. Plus, you have your college uniform on, and he looked to be in his thirties at least."

Lily frowned, not quite getting what he was saying. She swallowed quickly. "What do you mean?" she asked.

"You could be jail bait, Lily," Jake explained, obviously knowing what Nate meant.

"What? But I'm nearly eighteen."

"He wouldn't know that. College uniform should have made him think twice. You could be fifteen and just look older for all he knew," Josh pointed out. "I didn't see the man, not this morning or now, but if he's that old he shouldn't even look twice at you."

"It was coffee, not a suggestion to sleep with him," she rebutted, flummoxed by their reasoning. She knew they a point about her uniform and age, but he hadn't propositioned her, just been friendly.

"Lily, take it from another male, it's usually the same thing," Jake snorted.

"Lily, he was hitting on you," Matt said quietly. "If you're interested in him, then fair enough, but—"

"No." Nate cut him off sharply. "Matt! Don't tell her that! We don't know him from Adam. Why would a man that old be interested in a schoolgirl, Matt? That's just wrong on lots of levels."

"She's fucking beautiful." Jake spoke through a mouthful of pizza. "He'd have to be dead not to be interested in her."

Lily felt her face flush at the compliment he paid her.

"Well, yes, of course she's beautiful," Nate said, getting riled up. "But she still can't go off with a complete fucking stranger for coffee and whatever the hell else he wants from her!"

"He said he's renting the cottage opposite Lil's," Matt said. "Must be the one Mrs Johnston owns, the holiday home."

"I don't like him, Lily May!" Nate said. She heard him muttering something else under his breath. He was worried, that much was clear, and she didn't want him to worry about her.

"It's okay," she spoke up and turned around completely in her seat so she could see him. "I won't go for coffee with him. I don't know him, and he doesn't interest me."

"He doesn't interest you at all?" Josh asked, and again she got the impression her answer was important to them.

"No. He was good looking, yes, but his eyes were wrong."

She heard Nate grunt, but Matt spoke up. "What do you mean wrong?"

"They looked blank. I mean, almost dead somehow, as if he had… no soul." She frowned. "And now I'm being stupid." She shook her head. "He can't help his eyes, poor man."

"It's your gut instinct," Josh said, pointing his pizza crust at her. "Go with it; it rarely lets you down."

"I doubt he'd even give me another thought. He was probably just being friendly because he knows we're neighbours." Again, she heard Nate snort, but nothing else was said. Matt put his belt on, and she took her cue to turn around and belt up. She finished the last of her slice, licking her fingers clean.

"You still up for tomorrow, Lil?" Josh asked. Lily looked back at him, not sure what he meant.

"The quarry," Jake reminded her. "Swimming. It really will be one of the last chances we get this year, unless you happen to have a wetsuit?"

"No, I don't. I've never been scuba diving," she replied.

"We've got them because the sea is freezing, no matter what the time of year," Jake told her.

"We've still got our old ones in the attic," Josh spoke up. "Maybe one of them might fit you."

"We'll dig them out and bring one over tomorrow," Jake finished for him.

"Okay, thank you. I have a swimsuit, though," she said.

"A wetsuit over it will keep you warmer. Is it a bikini, or a full swimsuit?" Nate asked.

"Full one," she replied.

"Good, wear it under the wetsuit. You'll need old shoes that you can jump in with as well, don't go barefoot there," Matt spoke up. "We'll pick you up after lunch, okay?"

"Okay," she nodded, excited at the thought of going swimming with them. Matt pulled in by her gate, and she got out, dragging her bag with her. "Thanks for the lift."

"See you tonight," Matt called out.

"Yes. Bye!" She waved at them and ran up the path to the front door. She opened it, turned and waved again. She watched them wave back and then drive off before shutting her door.

"Lily?"

"Hey, Mum," she called, dropping her bag by the door and hanging her jacket up.

"Come and have a look, see what you think," her mother called from the living room.

Her mother was sitting cross legged on the floor, her sketch pad in her lap. "I managed to get a few more sketches done before the rain came down."

Lily moved forwards and knelt in front of her mother. She took the pad from her and smiled. "Is this Crowder Manor?" she asked. It was a three story, Georgian built house. It wasn't as large as she'd assumed when she heard manor, but it was beautiful. Vines covered one side of the house and wisteria hung over the entrance porch. Sweeping lawns hugged the gravel driveway. In the centre of the driveway was a round pond with an elegant fountain in the middle.

"Yes, locals still call it the vicarage; but Mr Crowder, Harold, doesn't like that. If you refer to it, call it a manor or Crowder Manor."

"What's he like?"

"He's a politician," her mother replied with a laugh. "No, that's mean. He's nice, quite polite, but formal. His wife June is lovely. Really friendly. You'll like her."

"It's brilliant, Mum." Lily handed the pad back to her.

"Thank you, darling. Did you have a good day?" she asked. "Did your friend get his glasses fixed?"

"He's picking them up Monday after school." She got to her feet. "Tomorrow we're going swimming at the quarry. Matt's picking me up after lunch."

"I need to go back to the manor, so that works well. Do they know about you?"

"Mum, it was Matt and Nate that were there when I had the seizure," she reminded her mother. "Besides, I'm sure it was just the stress from moving. I'm fine now."

"Take your phone with you just in case you need me."

"I will. I'm going to get some homework done before we leave." Lily got to her feet and dropped a kiss on top of her mother's head. "I'll wear the green dress, that do?"

"That one looks lovely on you," her mother replied, her pencil flying over the paper as she spoke.

Lily smiled at her mother's bent head, she would need to come down and remind her to get ready. When she started drawing or painting, she got lost in her own world, and time meant nothing to her. Lily went out, closing the door quietly.

Crowder Manor

Crowder Manor was exactly as her mother had drawn it. Except for the colour. The lawns were immaculately cut and a brilliant emerald green. Late summer flowers edged the borders of the lawn and around the fountain. The wisteria that draped over the entrance was no longer in bloom, but Lily could imagine how beautiful it would be when it flowered. Lily's mum parked their purple Mini around the side of the building. Her mother picked some of the flowers from their own garden; flowers Lily had no name for, and no interest in finding out. She liked looking at gardens but that was as close to gardening as she got.

The front door opened as they rounded the corner, and Matt came out. He was dressed in black slacks and a white shirt, the top three buttons undone. His hair was brushed and almost tamed, the front section was swept away from his eyes. He made her breath catch in her throat.

"Mrs Adair. Lily." He came over, a smile on his gorgeous face, his eyes on Lily's mum. There was a movement from the entrance and two more people came out. Lily could see where Matt got his looks from. His father was an older version of him. The only difference was the grey in his hair and the lines around his eyes. His smile was as engaging as his son's.

"Lynda, Lily, glad you could make it." Mr Crowder forward with his wife beside him. She was small, dark haired and looked nothing like Matt. But she could see Josh and Jake in her; it made her smile that she was more like her nephews than her own son.

"Lily." Her hand was shaken by Mr Crowder and then his wife, who insisted she call them June and Harold. June wrapped an arm around her mother's shoulders and led her towards the house with Harold, already talking to her about how excited she was after seeing the sketches.

"You look pretty, Lily," Matt shoved his hands into the pockets of his slacks. She was wearing her nicest dress, a bottle green fit and flare dress that ended just above her knees. It had a sweetheart neckline, three quarter length sleeves, and a black belt that encircled her waist. Black kitten heels completed the look.

She coloured up at his compliment. "Let's just hope it doesn't rain. I forgot my coat."

He laughed and indicated the front door with his head. "Come on, we've got a couple of minutes before dinner's ready. I'll show you 'round if you want."

"It's a lovely house, Matt," she said, falling into step with him.

"I like it. I've lived here all my life. After dinner, when your mum is taking her photos, I'll show you the grounds. The others will be up by then, I expect."

She stepped through the front door and sighed happily. It was like stepping into a Jane Austen movie; Georgian in its decorations, and in keeping with the age of the building.

"Is Captain Wentworth around here?" she asked, grinning at him. He laughed and shook his head.

"My mum will be pleased to hear you say that. It's the look she's aiming for."

"Well, you can tell her she's succeeded."

"And would Captain Wentworth make you swoon?" he asked, leaning in close to her, his mouth close to her ear, a wicked smirk tugging at his lips.

"I rather think he might." She laughed, and he aimed a shot to the heart, falling back from her.

"You mean to tell me, you won't swoon for me, but you'll swoon for a fictional character? Lily, I feel cheated."

"Oh, don't worry," she said teasingly. "Everyone knows fictional characters are the best. They won't let you down, and they're always there when you need them."

"Really?" He slid his arm around her shoulder and led her into a small room to the side. "Well, we're going to have our work cut out for us if we're to change your mind, Lily Flower. This is the office where the vicar wrote all his sermons. It's exactly as it was, nothing has been changed."

She looked around the small room in delight. There were paintings and embroidered bible passages on two of the walls, the third held a large painting of baby Jesus with Mary. A desk was situated under the window; a ledger lay on it, opened to a page filled with writing. An open Bible lay beside it. Lily could almost taste the history in the room, and it made her shiver with delight.

"Where is he now?" she asked.

"He died a long time ago. My great-great-grandfather bought the place well over a hundred years ago. His life story is a sordid tale of greed and bribery. I'll tell you one day," he said. "But only if you promise to behave."

"I always behave," she said with a laugh. He looked down at her, his hair falling into his eyes.

"Yes, I rather think you do. In that case, I'll amend it, I'll tell you if you promise to not behave."

"Matthew, we're going to sit down now, darling. Lynda would like to take her photos before she loses the light."

Matt turned at the sound of his mother's voice, but he didn't move his arm from around Lily's shoulders. Lily blushed, but his mother gave no indication that she noticed her son had his arm around a strange girl. Instead, she sent Lily a warm smile before going back the way she'd come.

"Come on then, Lily Flower. Let's hope that slice of pizza didn't ruin your appetite." He slid his arm from around her, caught her hand, and led her from the room.

Dinner passed quickly and comfortably. She was seated opposite Matt and beside her mother. At first, she'd been nervous, but between him and his parents, she soon relaxed. Her mother and June kept up the conversation, mostly about June's gardens and the prospect of painting the grounds in different seasons. Lily enjoyed listening to them. Mr Crowder was mostly quiet as he ate, seemingly content to let his wife do all the talking. Matt occasionally caught her eye over the table and winked at her or pulled a funny face when no one was looking. She had to keep wiping her mouth with her napkin to cover the laughter that kept trying to escape.

After they finished, her mother made her way out into the gardens, and Lily and Matt helped to clear the table for his mother. Once everything was put into the dishwasher in the pristine kitchen, Matt led her through the utility room and out into a boot room.

"What size feet do you have, Lily?" he asked, rummaging around in a giant bin that held all sort of shoes and wellington boots.

"Five," she replied.

"Ah, here you go then. Mum's a five. These should fit you." He turned and held out a pair of green wellingtons that looked well used.

"What about your mum?" she asked, not sure about borrowing them.

"What about her? She won't want them at the moment," he said with a chuckle. "She doesn't tend to wear her wellies around the house. Mud is hell to get out of the carpets apparently."

Lily rolled her eyes, laughing. "No, silly, I meant will she mind?" Lily asked, as he put them in front of her the right way around.

"No, of course not. I'd lend you my other pair, but they're an eleven and would fall off you."

She slid her shoes off, put the boots on, and then took the jacket that he held out to her. It swamped her, but it smelt like him so she wrapped it around herself and smiled at him. "Thanks. Is this one yours?"

He stepped forward, and taking the collars, he tugged them together until his hands were under her chin. "Yeah, and you look cute in my jacket," he murmured.

He bent his head quickly and before she knew what he was doing, he gently kissed her cheek where it dimpled. He let her go just as quickly, turned and opened the back door. Lily was thrown completely by the kiss; she lifted her fingers to her cheek, aware of the tingle where his lips had been. It was just a friendly kiss, but it took her breath away.

He looked back at her and the smile on his face widened slightly. "Come on, the rest of them will wonder where we are."

His words shook her out of her trance, and she quickly followed him out of the door. "Where are we going?" she asked in an effort to shrug off the way he made her feel.

"You'll see." He grinned at her, took a flashlight from his pocket, and handed it to her.

"Caving?" she asked, putting it into a pocket. "Because if so, I think I should add at this point that I'm not great with tight spaces."

"No, not caving," he reassured her. "There are caves along the shoreline but not on the grounds."

"Caves? Is that why the pub is called the Bootlegger?" she asked as they walked across the lawn towards the trees. "Were there smugglers here?"

"This is the Cornish coast, Lil. Most of it was used for smuggling. There are old paths that lead down the cliffs to caves below where contraband was stored. And there are hundreds of stories of wreckers and smugglers. It's fascinating stuff. I just wished local history was part of our A level course. I've been reading about it for years."

"This is my first time in Cornwall, but I've always loved reading stories about smuggling. I was hoping we'd be close to Bodmin Moor and the Jamaica Inn when Mum said we were coming to Cornwall."

"Stories aren't always accurate. For example, there are no documented accounts of wreckers." He stopped to help her climb over a fallen log, taking her hand in his and not letting go. "They didn't light fires or use lanterns to lure sailors to wreck; they used to douse them instead. If sailors saw a light that they were unfamiliar with, they tended to keep away from it, not head towards it."

"So lights would have warned them off, but putting them out could lead them onto rocks?"

"Exactly, if you're interested in reading about it, I have books you can look at. And I know Jonas has hundreds."

"Jonas? Who's Jonas?" she asked.

"Who? Oh, just a friend," he said vaguely. Lily got the impression he had said something he shouldn't and that whoever Jonas was, he didn't want her to know about him. She let it go. It was none of her business anyway.

They slowed down in their walking, and Lily enjoyed the feel of his hand around hers and the beauty of the trees around them. In the dying light of the day, it was starting to grow darker, but the sound of the wind teasing the leaves and the birds singing their last chorus before sleep made it seem enchanted somehow. Moss, twigs, and leaves lay under foot, she could see where some of the trees were starting to change colour. Autumn was going to be early this year, and it looked like it was going to be a beautiful one.

"It's very beautiful here," she said quietly, soaking in the atmosphere.

"I like it. These woods go all the way behind where you live. There's a shortcut through here to the village. I'll show it to you when we have more light. The others use it all the time."

"Are they meeting us somewhere?" With his help, she picked her way over another fallen branch.

"Yeah, we usually end up here most evenings." They came to a divide in the path, and he turned them right. Lily caught the silver flash of a river up ahead, and she could hear it now as well.

"Am I honoured then?" she asked with a grin. "Or do you bring all the new girls here?" She was teasing him, but she saw him frown and then look a little surprised.

"Well, now you mention it," he said, and scratched at the back of his head. "You're the only person we've ever brought here."

His words caught her by surprise. She looked up at him, not sure whether to believe him or not.

"Well, it's about bloody time," came a laugh. "We were beginning to think you'd forgotten."

She could hear them, but she couldn't see anyone as she looked around her, still holding Matt's hand. She saw a flash of movement to her left and the twins came through the trees with Nate behind them. They each had flashlights in their hands.

"Where on earth are we going that's going to need flashlights?" Lily asked in surprise.

"You'll see," Nate said, walking towards the river. "Hurry up, the sun is going down, and you need to see this in the daylight if you can."

"See what?" she tried asking one of the twins, not certain yet which was which; as per usual, they were dressed identically in black jeans and black jackets. But all he did was smirk at her.

"Get off!" Matt shouted, pulling free from her when the other twin started to stuff leaves down the back of his neck. It started an all-out war between the three of them, and not wanting leaves down her neck she rushed ahead to catch up with Nate. He shook his head, and catching her hand, he led her along the edge of the river. It was mostly clear of trees now and the sun was still high enough to make the water gleam as it flowed over rocks towards the sea.

"It's lovely here." Peace settled over her; in her. A peace she'd never experienced before.

"It's good for fishing, and further down there's a slower part that's great for swimming in. We've got a couple of rope swings set up in the trees. It's getting cold now, but next summer we can chuck you in." He grinned at her, and she started to laugh. But then it sank in what he'd said, and she looked away hurriedly.

"I probably won't be here next summer, Nate." She tried to sound casual about it but didn't quite succeed.

"Your mum will move on?" he asked.

"As soon as my exams are over. If she's finished the paintings."

She heard him swear under his breath, and then he was turning her to grip both of her hands.

"Lily May, you'll be eighteen, nearly nineteen, when that happens. You can't spend your entire life attached to your mum's apron strings. You don't have to go where she goes. You can do whatever the hell you want to do. If you want to go to Uni, go. If you don't, don't."

"Nate, I can't be left on my own," she reminded him, and she saw him pull a face as he'd obviously forgotten.

"But there must be hundreds of people without a family that have epilepsy. She won't always be here, Lily May."

"I know." She pulled her hands free from his and crossed to pick up a stone, throwing it into the water. "Before we came here, I was fine. I didn't question it, I just went with the flow. I never regretted leaving anywhere, and I even looked forward to discovering new places. But now?" She threw another stone in, watching the splash it made. "The other morning when I was late? She'd just told me that we were moving again. That she was going to give the down payment back to Mr Crowder and leave for Ireland." She laughed, but it wasn't humorous. She picked up more stones, sending them into the river. "I panicked. The thought of leaving here was awful. I've never felt more at home than I have here, and when she said we were going? I begged her to let us stay. This place is not good for me. I'm getting too attached; we will move, and I will go with her, because there's nothing else for me to do."

"There's always something else you can do, Lily."

She turned, hearing Matt's voice. All four of them stood together, listening to her, concern on their faces but no pity. And she was glad of that.

"Don't say anything to your dad, please, Matt. She's agreed to stay till she's finished."

"I won't say anything," he promised her, and she nodded her thanks. Sadness tugged at her, making her stomach hurt.

"There are a few months before you need to worry about anything. And I think being here is exactly what you need, Lily

May," Nate said firmly. "Come on, we're running out of light." He indicated with his head for her to follow him. The twins fell into step either side of her while Matt went ahead to walk with Nate.

"You're going to love this place" Josh told her. She kept her hands in the pockets of Matt's jacket, clutching the flashlight. They were all free and easy with their hand holding, and because none of them showed any reaction to seeing the others do it, it told her that they viewed her as friend and nothing more. She should protect herself from falling for them, because she was sure it would be an easy thing to do. And despite what they said, she knew that when her mother moved from here, and she would, she was going as well. Because that was the way it had always been, and always would be for the foreseeable future.

"Here we are," Matt called back. She looked up to see a three story, stone building at the edge of the river. It looked like an old barn, with the large windows further up for the hay bales.

"A hay barn?" she asked. The stone steps that led up the side to the third floor had no railing to hold on to. "Anyone fallen to their death from there?"

"It's not a hay barn, Lily May, and no one has ever fallen to their death," Nate told her as he disappeared around the corner that edged the river. "But be careful how you walk here!" he called out. "It gets close to the river in some places."

She looked at Josh, but he just smirked at her and indicated with his hand for her to go ahead of him. She couldn't keep the grin from her face as she went to the corner of the building. The twins fell in behind her as she picked her way through the stones and nettles, her hand on the stones of the wall for balance. She could hear a loud rumbling noise that meshed in with the rushing water of the river. She realised now that they were showing her a waterwheel. She rounded the corner and looked up.

Her head spun and her knees buckled, her hand scraped painfully against the wall as she went down. Hands caught her under her arms before she could hit the ground.

She'd seen this waterwheel before. She'd been here before, of that she was certain, and it slammed into her like a hammer to her head.

"Shit, did you trip?" She was vaguely aware of Nate out of her peripheral vision, but her gaze was locked on the waterwheel ahead of her, slowly turning as water was channelled onto it via an aqueduct. Her vision narrowed to the turning of the wheel. Images slammed into her head, noises in her ears. She could hear a child screaming, two children screaming. One child being pulled towards the water that churned under the wheel, another valiantly trying to reach it before falling in himself. Both children struggled desperately but the pull was too strong for them and they were dragged beneath the ever-turning wheel. She stumbled forwards frantically, she had to get to them before they drowned. Something was holding her back, shouting in her ears as she stumbled and fell to the ground. She clawed her way forwards, desperately trying to get to them before it was too late, but something heavy was holding her down. Hands on her waist and legs refused to let her go.

"Lily! Lilith!"

She heard her name being roared, then she was lifted from the ground. She groaned as her vision went hazy and her head lolled back against someone warm.

"It's okay, Lily. It's okay, we've got you. Nate, get her onto her side!"

She felt the hard ground underneath her as she was rolled onto her side. Her vision cleared, the grass came into sharp focus. Pain wracked through her skull, making her close her eyes. She could hear voices murmuring low around her, but confusion was making her thoughts jumbled. She had seen those children, had heard the screaming. But now? Now she knew that they couldn't have been there at all. The boys would have seen them too, done something to help them. Instead they were worried about her. That told her she'd been… what? Hallucinating? But she'd seen that waterwheel before, she knew she had. She'd seen it when she'd had a seizure on Monday. Fear filled every pore. What was wrong with her?

"It can be anything up to half an hour."

"That was not a fucking epileptic fit!"

"We don't know that, Josh."

"We fucking do! They don't try to throw themselves head first into the river screaming! They jerk about, and then are completely out of it for twenty minutes!"

"Jake!"

"We're right! That was not normal!"

Lily heard their words clearly. She opened her eyes and nausea rose from her stomach. She took deep breaths and struggled to her knees. Pain shot through her skull.

"Hey, hey, slow down, Lily. Slow down." Matt's calm voice was in her ear, but she shrugged off his hand on her back. She was confused, frightened. They thought she was mad, and horror filled her that they might be right.

"I'm sorry," she mumbled and stumbled to her feet, aware of his hands helping her up. "I have to go now." She didn't wait, didn't look back, she just stumbled her way towards what she hoped was the path back. Humiliation warred with the fear filling her.

"Lily! Wait!"

She heard them calling her, but she couldn't face them, too scared to even look back at them. She just kept going until her way was blocked by two identical bodies.

"Stop! Stop panicking, Lily May," Nate's voice was firm, and she found herself listening to him, but she still couldn't bring herself to look at any of them.

"Just sit down for a moment."

"I need to go home." The pain in her head was worsening, and she still felt sick.

"We'll walk you back in a few minutes," Matt said. "Just sit down for a moment first, Lily."

She felt him put his hand on her arm and tug her gently to a fallen log. She sank down onto it, and hugged her arms around her knees, keeping her eyes on the toes of her boots.

"Lily, sweetheart, look at me." Nate crouched in front of her, but she didn't want to acknowledge any of them. There was too much going through her mind. She kept seeing the children by the water, hearing their screams. She shivered and closed her eyes, trying to banish the images but it just made them stronger. What was wrong with her?

"What happened, Lily?" She felt a warm body settle on each side of her, and two arms snaked around her waist. "Did you have a seizure?" It was Matt's voice she heard; he had crouched next to Nate.

"I... think so." She lifted a hand to rub her forehead and saw how badly she was shaking. "I think I hallucinated... or something." It was the something that froze her heart in fear.

"Tell us what you saw," Nate whispered. He placed his hand on her knee as Matt caught her shaking hand in his.

"I... I've seen the waterwheel before. On Monday, when I had the seizure."

"And what did you see today when you saw the waterwheel?" Nate's voice was low, calm, and it curled around her, relaxing her slightly. The body heat from the twins was helping, pressing into her tightly, arms around her waist. She was surrounded by them, and it helped centre her.

Lily drew in a shaky breath. "Two children. They fell in and were being sucked under the waterwheel." She closed her eyes and dragged her hand from Matt's to cover her face with both hands. She was terrified of what was happening to her now. Maybe there was a brain tumour that was causing her seizures to change. Dread made her break out in a cold sweat.

"Hey, it's okay." Josh lifted his hand and began rubbing circles on her back.

"No, it's not okay. It's not normal, you said it yourself," she murmured. "Maybe there's something wrong with my brain. I've had MRI scans and CAT scans. What if they missed something?"

"Lily." Nate reached forward and drew her hands away from her face. He bent forward till she had to look at him. "I researched it, Lily. When I realised you had fits, I researched it in case you had one with us. We needed to know what to do. One of the things I read was that some people with epilepsy hallucinate."

"Really?" She grasped his words, looking straight at him. It was almost dark but the blue of his eyes seemed to glow somehow. "They do?"

"Yes. I'm surprised no one told you." He smiled at her. "The main thing is that you are alright. You're fine, do you understand? You're not going mad. You're perfectly sane."

"We didn't mean it wasn't normal," Josh spoke up. "We just meant that we weren't expecting…" He stopped when Nate looked at him, his head tilted slightly.

"Do you have a headache, Lily?" Matt asked softly, and she nodded. Relief flooded through her at Nate's words. She didn't know about hallucinating; she had never been told about it. But then nothing had happened before that would warrant any of the doctors telling her.

"Lily! Lily!"

Lily heard her mother calling her name, and she rubbed her hands over her face.

"Get a good sleep and you'll be fine in the morning, Lily May. You'll need it for swimming."

"Are you sure you want to chance that?" She snorted, rubbing at her forehead. "I don't seem to have a very good track record around you all."

"I think we can handle whatever you throw at us." Matt chuckled. "Life won't be boring with you."

She shook her head deprecatingly and got to her feet when she heard her mother call out again.

"Over here, Mrs Adair!" Nate called out and then turned to Lily. "Do you want her to know? Or will it just worry her?"

She frowned. She'd never hidden a seizure from her mother before, but that was because she was usually there when they happened or was called to pick up the pieces when it happened when she was at school. But she also knew that if she told her now it would just worry her. It was unusual for her to have two seizures so close together. While Lily was sure it was just stress, she knew her mother would blame herself.

"I'll tell her later," Lily said. Nate smiled, and she had the impression that he was pleased with her decision.

"There you are, is everything okay?" Her mother came down the path, June with her.

"Hello, boys!" June gave a bright smile when she saw all of them.

"Aunt June, Mrs Adair, we were just showing Lily the waterwheel," Nate said. He stepped towards her and kissed his aunt's cheek, quickly followed by the twins.

"Lynda, these are my nephews; Nate, and the twins, Josh and Jake." June introduced them to her mother. It gave Lily a few more minutes to gather her wits about her.

"Hello, boys. It's nice to meet you."

The boys introduced themselves, and her mother laughed when the twins bowed to her, big grins on their faces.

"How do people tell you apart?" she asked them.

"With difficulty," June said dryly before they could reply. "I've known them since they were born, and I still get it wrong, don't I boys?"

"Yes, you do, Aunty," Josh said, and Lynda laughed, shaking her head.

"We'd best be getting on. It was nice to meet you, Mrs Adair," Nate said. "Pick you up after lunch tomorrow, Lily, okay?"

She nodded and regretted it when her head thumped painfully making her wince.

"Are you okay, Lily?" Her mother picked up on it instantly.

"Headache," she murmured.

"We'd best get home, Lily. We've only just moved in, and it's been a stressful few weeks, June."

"I can imagine," June agreed, and they began to walk back towards the manor.

It was almost dark under the trees and Lily couldn't see well at all. The boys drew out flashlights, and it helped to pick out their way, but it seemed that every twig in the path was enough to cause Lily to stumble.

Matt moved into her side and put his arm around her waist. He bent to put his mouth to her ear.

"Lean on us, Lily. We'll look after you, I promise." His words seemed deeper than just leaning on him to stop herself from falling, but her head was too muddled to do anything but retreat into numbness.

By the time he helped her into the car, the others had disappeared, and it was just him and his mother. She was dimly aware of him sliding his fingers across her forehead as he stepped back from the car. She sank into sleep before he'd even closed the car door.

"Lily, sweetheart, I'm sorry. I can't carry you in, darling. Not these days."

Her mother's voice in her ear woke her up. She opened her eyes, disorientated for a few seconds. The interior light illuminated the car enough for her to see her mother leaning towards her. She licked her lips and stretched. It felt like she'd been asleep for hours, when in reality it was probably only a few minutes.

"How's your head? Take some paracetamol when you get in."

Lily frowned. Her headache had gone completely, not even leaving the twinges she sometimes got after a seizure.

"It's gone." Relief flooded through her that she wouldn't have to suffer through another migraine.

"Gone?" Her mother's voice was confused. "How can it just go?"

"Maybe I slept it off." Lily undid her belt and got out of the car.

"You did go out like a light," she agreed. "Maybe it was the stress of your mother meeting your boyfriend, when you hadn't even told her you had one," she added slyly.

"What?" Lily hesitated in opening the door to look around at her mother. She grinned and got out.

"Matthew."

Lily jumped out, closed her door and glared over the roof at her mother as she locked the car. "He's a friend, Mum. Just a friend."

"Of course, dear. June is as happy as I am. She likes you."

"Mum!"

"What?" Her mother swept up the path and unlocked the door, the little light above the front door lighting her way.

"He's just a friend!"

"Of course he is, that's the best way to start a relationship," she called out, and went in laughing.

Lily rolled her eyes and shook her head as she started towards the cottage. There would be no convincing her mother.

"Lilith."

Lily whirled, certain she'd heard her name. She looked up and down the badly illuminated lane; only one street light lit the area and that was further down towards the green. She could see no one.

"Come in and stop sulking," her mother called out.

Lily shrugged, it must have been her mother. She stopped in her doorway and looked up and down the lane, but there was still no sign of anyone. She looked over at the cottages opposite. Lights were on in the windows at either end, but the one in the middle looked dark and unlived in. A movement caught her eye and she peered into the darkness of the door. A glow of red that disappeared seconds later startled her until she realised it was the end of a cigarette. Someone stood in the door smoking.

"Lilith! You're letting in the cold air, shut the door!" her mother shouted. She saw the door open and whoever it was went inside.

She closed her own door and realised she still had Matt's jacket on as well as his mother's boots. She would return them tomorrow when he picked her up.

"Lily, are you okay?" Her mum stepped into the light of the hallway from the living room. "Are you sure it was just a headache tonight?"

This was her chance, she could tell her mother that her seizures were changing again. That hallucinations were now part of the deal. But something held her back from saying anything.

"Yeah, just a headache." She shrugged out of his jacket. The moment she set it on the coat peg she missed the feel of it surrounding her, missed the smell that was particular to Matt.

"I think I'll get an early night," Lily murmured, and pried the boots off her feet. She kissed her mother goodnight and made her way upstairs.

Hallucinations. She didn't know what to think of it yet, and it was one of the reasons she'd held back on telling her mother. If she shut her eyes, she could still hear the screams, see the boy try valiantly to reach the other child before falling in himself and being mercilessly pulled under the wheel by the flow of the water. She wasn't sure how much she could take if her seizures started adding full technicolour drama like that.

But she still didn't want to tell her mother just yet. When her seizures changed from absent seizures to tonic-clonic, her mother had been distraught for days. It had triggered a move as well. It was one of the rare times that her mother uprooted her mid school year.

Lily didn't want to move again. She wanted to stay here, she wanted to stay with her friends. Friends, who not only accepted her seizures, but cared enough to find out what to do if she had one when she was with them. She'd never had friends who had done that before. She would tell her mother only if she had to, and not before.

Jonas

None of them had gone home, instead they'd crept up to Matt's room to wait for him to come up from saying goodbye to Lily.

"That wasn't an epileptic fit," Josh stated as soon as the door shut behind Matt.

"No, it wasn't," agreed Nate. He was sitting on the end of Matt's bed. He leant forward, stretching his arms along his legs. "But if it wasn't, what the hell was it?"

"Not to mention what she said she saw." Jake shuddered.

"Just give me a moment. I remember something. I'll be back in a minute." Matt left the room, shutting the door behind him.

"She just went down," Nate murmured, clasping his hands together, his hair falling into his face.

"She struggled to get free," Jake said. "We weren't expecting her to launch herself forward like that." His worry showed clearly.

"She was trying to crawl across the ground like she was fucking possessed," Josh agreed. He slung his arm around Jake's neck, and they sat down on Matt's window seat.

The door opened again, and Matt came in, his normally cheerful face was sombre, and his eyes guarded.

"I think I know what she saw." Matt shut the door behind him. He had a brown book in his hand that looked like an extremely old ledger.

"What?" Nate sat up as Matt crossed to the bed and set the book down on it.

"This is the diary of the last vicar that lived here, and these"—he brought forward a grainy photograph that was clearly

Victorian in age—"are his children, Charles and Martha. There are several entries from the beginning of July 1888 and onwards that are sad. He had two children, these two. They both drowned by the mill, but it doesn't give any details on how it happened, other than the children's nanny found them slightly downstream. The vicar's wife went into shock and never recovered. She was sent to an asylum four months later. My great-great grandfather saw an opportunity and took it, that's how he got this place at half the normal sum from the church. I remembered reading this years ago."

"So she's not epileptic." Nate rubbed his forehead, his breath leaving him on a sigh.

"Fucking hell." Jake's voice was hushed. "So what are we saying? She's a Medium? She can see the fucking dead? Jesus Christ!"

"No." Matt shook his head. "Or at least I don't think so." He looked at Nate for confirmation.

"What the fuck are we saying?" Jake demanded.

"I think Lily may be a Seer," Nate spoke up. He moved to push his glasses up his nose and gave a noise of disgust when he realised they weren't there.

"A Seer?" Josh repeated the word as if he'd never heard it. "A Visionary? You think she's getting visions?"

"I think we need to talk to Jonas." Nate looked at Matt.

"Agreed," Matt said quietly. "Now?"

"Now." Nate nodded. "We need to be on top of this by the time we pick her up tomorrow."

"And if he says we need to stay away from her?" Jake asked doubtfully.

"We tell him to go fuck himself," Nate snapped. "She thinks she's epileptic and she's clearly not! She needs us."

"Yes, she does," Matt agreed.

"She's ours now, whether she knows it or not, Jacob," Josh said.

"Ours?" Matt looked at him, one eyebrow lifted. "You think you're the only one with a connection to her? She's not yours."

"Not now." Nate got to his feet. "Let's just get to Jonas."

***

Nate rang the doorbell several times and then knocked impatiently. A light came on behind the frosted glass door, and it was opened by a sleepy looking man in his late forties who frowned, drawing his dressing gown around him tighter.

"What do you lot want?" he inquired. "And at this time of night?" He didn't wait for a reply, he just turned and started to walk back into the house. They trooped in after him, Jake brought up the rear, locking the door behind him.

Jonas led them into his living room and slumped into his armchair. He rubbed at his face, watching as they collapsed down into the various sofas and armchairs that were around the room. Books and papers were stacked everywhere. They were on the floor, and on the coffee table which was set in front of an open, unlit fire. Bookcases lined three of the walls and were stuffed full of books and magazines. The house was Victorian, and although there was electricity, all the lights were still the old-fashioned gas lamps. Lamps which Jonas controlled with a snap of his fingers.

"Okay, who's died?" he drawled and crossed his pyjama clad legs. His tartan slipper slid down his foot and dangled from the end of his toes, but he made no move to put it back on properly. His hair was a sandy blonde colour and all over the place from being asleep. Shrewd blue eyes, which caught more than they missed, watched the boys. His voice was a slow rumble that held people's attention without him even trying.

"No one," Nate said. "We have a question."

"You do?" Jonas slapped his lips together and folded his arms. "If it's to do with schoolwork, I'll turn you all into toads. You do realise what time it is, don't you?"

"It can't wait," Nate said and got up. He crossed to where a globe stood on the desk under the curtain covered window. He spun it gently, a frown between his eyes. "It's about a girl."

"A girl?" Jonas shook his head. "I'm thinking it must be more than hormones at question here. What's she done?"

"We don't know. She's only just moved here and has epileptic fits, or at least she thinks she does." Nate watched Jonas's reaction and wasn't surprised when he saw him sit forward slightly, uncrossing his legs. A cat slinked its way between Josh's legs, and he bent to pick it up, scratching it behind its ears, making it purr contentedly.

"Start at the beginning," Jonas commanded, and for the next twenty minutes they told him everything. He listened carefully, his eyes on the cat in Josh's arms.

"By her own admission, her fits have changed," Josh finished with a sigh. Jonas sat back in his seat and lit the fire with a casual flick of his fingers. He stared into the flames as he thought, not saying anything.

"She only saw colours before coming here, now she's seeing actual events," Matt spoke up.

"Is she seeing dead people?" Jake asked. "Well, we know she saw dead people, but is she a Seer or a Medium?"

"I'd like to meet her," Jonas said. "I'd say from what you've described she's a Seer. Traditionally they don't come into their full powers before they're eighteen, but it sounds like she's been having breakthroughs all these years without even knowing. When is she eighteen?"

"Twenty-ninth of this month," Matt told him.

"Odd for her to suddenly be experiencing full visions before then. But you may have caused that, especially if you're causing her to experience an emotional connection with you. Is one of you her boyfriend? Are you physical?" Jonas asked, looking between each of them.

Each of them started to say that they weren't physical with her, but that they liked her. Jonas held up a hand for silence.

"You all like her, but you're just friends?" he asked and watched four heads nod reluctantly.

"Oh, boy." He snorted with laughter, rubbing at his eyes again. "Trust you lot to complicate things."

"We hardly complicated things," Nate said, getting defensive. "We've all agreed to be her friend."

"Whatever. You'll need to sort that out yourselves. Bring her here tomorrow to meet me. If she's a Seer and she has no idea, she's going to need help controlling it."

"So she could be fae, like us?" Josh asked him,

"Seers aren't technically fae. They come from another bloodline; one much darker than our own. They have their roots in a darker magic than ours, I've heard it said they are the human descendants of the first woman Lilith, but I've never been able to find the proof."

"Oh, fuck," Josh snorted, and covered his eyes with his hand. "That's ironic," he muttered.

"What's ironic?" Jonas asked. "And watch your language!"

"Her full name is Lilith," Nate said quietly, and Jonas stared at him.

"Ironic indeed," Jonas replied. "Their roots are lost in history, much like our own. All I do know is that their roots aren't fae, but witch."

"She's a bloody witch?" Jake shot out and thumped his head against the sofa.

"No, if she's a Seer, then she's a Seer, not a witch," Jonas corrected him. "To have a Witch Seer is extremely rare. There would be other indications as well, she'd be able to do things that she couldn't really explain. And she wouldn't be confused thinking she had epilepsy. She would just know she was different, like you all did, even though you didn't know why."

"What do we do?" Nate asked. "To help her?"

"Bring her to me, let me make absolutely sure she's a Seer and not epileptic with a good imagination. We can go from there." Jonas stood up. "You're all welcome to camp out here if you want. Lord knows it won't be the first time. I'm knackered; the little devils get worse each year. Or is it that I just get older?" he mused, making his way to the door.

He hesitated in the doorway and looked back at them. "I've known you boys a long time now. You share everything, but you can't share a girl," he said quietly. "You'll need to think on that." He went out of the room and then stuck his head back around the door, a wicked smile on his lips. "Unless of course you don't mind polyamory. Goodnight boys; if you're up before me, leave me at least one egg and don't drink all the milk this time, please. Mysty, c'mon," he added. The cat leapt from Josh's arms and trotted towards her owner. He closed the door, leaving them staring at each other.

"What the fuck is polyamory?" Jake muttered, digging out his phone from his jean pockets and bringing up a search app.

"You got that from what he said?" Nate demanded, making Jake look up at him.

"What? I thought we were pretty sure she's a Seer? He's going to double check, but he hasn't told us anything new."

"Except that she's not fae," Matt pointed out, rubbing a hand down his face. "I'm knackered as well; it was an absolute nightmare watching her flip like that."

"Matt, send out a group text to the mums letting them know where we are," Nate spoke up. "I'm too tired to drag myself back to the village. Let's crash here."

"Well, bugger me." Jake suddenly chuckled, shoving his phone under Josh's nose. He took it and started to read.

"What?" Nate demanded.

"There's a name to what we've been planning since we realised girls weren't as gross as we first thought." Jake chuckled again. "Polyamorous, like polygamy but reversed for us."

"You mean one man and several girls in a relationship?" Matt asked in surprised.

"Yeah, but it's one girl and several men," Josh said, and lifting his hand he did a fist bump with Jake.

"What the fuck are you two on about?" Nate snapped, feeling frustrated as well as tired.

"We decided years ago that we were going to find a girl that would settle with both of us at the same time," Josh said and handed the phone back to his twin.

"You can't share the same girl!" Nate exclaimed, rubbing his forehead tiredly.

"Why not?" Jake demanded. "Think about it. If we both had girlfriends, they might not get on together. If they're constantly fighting with each other how will we all live together? They might pull us apart as brothers."

"We made a pact years ago, a blood pact that nothing will ever separate us," Josh added. "Not time, not distance, and not a girl. The best way for us is to find a girl who will share us."

"So you two really are okay with sharing Lily?" asked Matt incredulously. "Well, fuck you, she might not want you two! She already feels something with me, I can tell."

"She reacts to me, too!" Nate shot to his feet. "I'm not standing back for you lot."

"Hold on, hold on." Josh jumped to his feet, followed quickly by Jake. "We thought you spouted all that shit about being her friend, not pushing her. Have you put the moves on her after telling us to hold back?"

"No, I haven't put the moves on her! But I think she feels something for me, too. I think if I kissed her, she'd respond. I've held her hand, stroked her cheek. And she liked it."

"I've held her hand, too," Matt said to Nate. "And kissed her cheek. She responded to that. I saw it in her eyes."

"Fuck you!" Josh spat, his voice rising. "She's our girl! We saw her first! You can't get all on it with her like that!"

"Your girl?" Matt and Nate turned to them, anger on their faces. "She's not your girl! You can't claim she's yours just because you saw her first!" Nate shouted.

"We really like her, but you're both just all about lust because she's pretty. We want more than just a one-night stand with her," Jake said sharply, his hands clenched into fists at his side.

"So do I!" Matt snapped. "I want more than that, and it isn't just lust, Jake."

"But you never date them beyond one-night stands," Nate sneered.

"Once!" Matt yelled. "I had a one-night stand once, and you lot think I'm the next Casanova. I was with Connie for six months! Six months before she dropped me for that loser!"

"Rebound!" Jake and Josh shouted at the same time, pointing at him. "You don't really like Lily, it's rebound from Connie still!"

"Fuck off!" Matt shouted. The door slammed behind them, making them turn to see Jonas standing in the doorway, Mysty in his arms. She hissed at them, her ears back.

"Will you lot shut up or get out!" he snapped, not happy at all. "You'll have Mrs Polden from next door complaining again."

"She's deaf," Nate snapped, glaring at Matt.

"Well, I'm not!" Jonas replied. "Look, I could hear every word you shouted at each other. And there's one thing your tiny brains have forgotten."

"What?" Matt asked, skimming his hands through his hair and sending it all over the place.

"That if she has any sense she won't want any of you anyway! You're all arguing over who gets her, boys, but the poor girl might not want to be got!"

"Shit." Nate deflated as he realised the truth in Jonas's words. She was desperate for friends that was sure, but that didn't mean that she wanted anything but friendship with them.

"Exactly. Now, please, shut up and let me sleep," he said firmly. He went back out, closing the door behind him. He opened it again and stuck his head around the door. "And I meant it about the milk. If it's all gone when I get up, I will never let you set foot over my threshold again!" He shut the door, and they were left staring at each other still.

"Shit, we've let happen what we swore would never happen," Matt muttered and slumped down onto the sofa, his legs apart and his hands in his hair.

"We've let something get between us," Nate agreed, and dropped into Jonas's armchair. The fire was still lit, and the heat was too much. He snapped his fingers, and it went out.

"You two have," Josh snorted, and slapped his hand on Jake's back. "We're quite happy with sharing her. It's nothing more than we hoped would happen anyway."

"Yeah, but that was between the two of you," Nate pointed out, toeing off his shoes and propping his feet on the coffee table. "There's us now as well. Look, Jonas was right, we have no idea what she would want. She may not want any of us."

"So we still stick with the friendship?" Matt asked unhappily.

"It'll have to be if she doesn't want you as anything more than a friend," Nate said quietly and rubbed his eyes. He swore when he dislodged a contact lens. He stood up, took both of them out, and set them on the mantelpiece above the fire.

"It's going to have to be good enough for all of us if she only wants us as friends," Nate said, his eyes watering as he sat back down.

"Hypothetically speaking," Matt said slowly and they all looked at him. "If she likes us all, agrees to date us all, but couldn't choose who she wanted a serious relationship with, what would we do?"

No one said anything. Matt closed his eyes and stretched out along the sofa he was sitting on. Josh and Jake laid themselves out on the other sofa, turning on their sides and facing outwards, pressed together tightly.

"It's been less than a week, and she's all I can think of. It's stupid, I know it is. Completely unrealistic, but I like her a lot," Matt murmured into the cushions.

"It's not just you," Jake murmured. "Perhaps Jonas has it all wrong and she is a witch, casting some sort of spell over us."

"For what reason?" Nate snorted, putting a cushion behind his head.

"Because she knows we're awesome and can't choose already?" Josh suggested.

"Well, I'm awesome," Matt muttered, half asleep. "You lot are passable."

"Fuck you," Josh murmured. "We're going to have to play this one by ear. To be honest, there's one other thing that we've forgotten in all this."

"What?" Jake asked.

"We're going to have to tell her what she is," Josh answered him. "That's going to blow her mind. She won't even be thinking of how great we all are."

"Oh, bugger," Nate grunted. "That is not going to be easy. I'm voting for letting Jonas deal with it."

"That's a cop out, Nate." Matt lifted his head, his eyes already bleary from tiredness.

"Nope, that's self-preservation. She's going to flip out on him, but we'll be there to pick up the pieces and help her cope."

"Point," Matt agreed, his head flopping back down. "I can help her deal with it."

"We all can," Nate said and shifted on the armchair. "Has he made this smaller?"

"Shut up and come over here," Matt muttered and turned to face the back of the sofa, leaving enough space for Nate to lie on his side. "Just face outwards, back to back."

"She's going to come between us," Nate murmured as he got up and then settled down in front of Matt, facing the room. He snapped his fingers and the gas lamps went out, leaving them in darkness.

"Only if we let her," Josh spoke up. "You two are our family. It's not a huge stretch of the imagination to share her with you all."

"Have you really decided to do that with a girl? You never said anything before," Matt muttered.

"We didn't know what you would think," Jake murmured, his voice rough with sleep. "It just seems natural to us."

"You do know you're not one person, don't you?" Nate said dryly, but neither of them answered him, just sniggered quietly.

Peace settled over the room, the clock on the wall ticked, and the walls creaked around them, but no other sounds were heard as they fell asleep.

Sharing

"You left me some milk; colour me impressed," Jonas drawled, coming into the kitchen, Mysty ahead of him, tail in the air.

"And we made you breakfast," Nate said, turning with a frying pan in his hand. He slid eggs and bacon onto an empty plate at the small table and then slid the pan into the sink. It sizzled as the heat of the pan hit the warm water, steam rising from the bowl.

"You can move in, boys." Jonas sat at the table, pulling the plate towards him and picking up a fork. "If you promise not to kill each other at midnight again."

"We didn't even come to blows," Matt said from the other side of the table, hidden behind the newspaper he was reading. "We were far too tired. Thanks for the loan of your sofas."

"You didn't even make it to the bedroom?" Jonas asked, with a roll of his eyes. "Why did I put beds in there if you won't even get that far? Do you kids realise what an excellent library or study that room would make?"

"We've made it that far before," Nate pointed out, scrubbing at the pan. "And we probably will again."

"So, if you haven't killed the twins and buried them at the bottom of my garden, where are the little miscreants?"

The back door opened on cue and they came in. Bags of shopping in their hands.

"Did you miss us?" Josh asked happily, setting milk, eggs, bacon, and a loaf of bread on the side.

"Like a hole in the head," Nate said, and flicked water at him from the sink.

"As badly as you'd miss your mouth? Nate, we love you too, buddy." Jake put him in a headlock and ruffled his hair affectionately before landing a big kiss on the top.

"Fuck off! I haven't had my vaccinations yet," Nate roared, his voice muffled under Jake's arm.

"Language! So what are you all doing today?" Jonas asked loudly, pushing his fork handle against the edge of the newspaper to get Matt to hold it straighter so he could read the sports on the back page.

"We're taking Lily swimming at the quarry," Matt murmured, and turned the page.

"He'll never get another season playing like that," Jonas snorted, cutting into his bacon. "Well, I'll be here all day, so bring her over whenever you're ready."

Matt closed up the paper and Jonas glared at him, picked it up, and concentrated on the back page again.

"About that," Matt said slowly, and Jonas looked up. One eyebrow rose as he chewed his bacon. "What are we going to tell her?"

"Let me play that by ear," Jonas said, wiping his mouth on a napkin. "I want to see just how much she knows already."

"She's clueless," Matt said, running a hand through his hair.

"So you say," Jonas drawled casually, and finished up his eggs.

"What do you mean by that?" Nate demanded.

"Just that I want to make sure she is what we think she is before we leap to any conclusions."

"You think she knows? You think she's playing us?" Josh asked quietly.

"I have no idea, and I won't until I meet her. Go! Swim in ridiculously cold water and bring her in later." He dismissed them with a wave of his hand. "Give me a little bit of peace to think as well."

Nate dried his hands on the towel as Matt scraped his chair back and got up.

"We'll bring her in about three-ish," Nate said, opening the back door. Jonas waved a hand at him, his attention back on the sports section of the paper. They went out, closing the door behind them and crossed to where Matt's Land Rover was parked beside the classic MG Roadster that belonged to Jonas.

"I need to know something before we pick up Lily." Matt stopped by the door and folded his arms over his chest. "Last night we were all stressed and knackered. What are we going to do? I'm serious about her being my girl. I'm just putting that out there for you."

"I am too," Nate said, and looked over at the twins.

"So are we, you know that already," Josh said, folding his arms. Jake moved to stand next to him, his stance identical to his twin as he watched Nate and Matt.

"So what do we do? Fight for her? Pistols at dawn?" Matt sighed heavily. "We can't let her come between us." He gestured at the defensive stances they'd taken. "But that's exactly what we're doing. We can't let this happen. We swore we'd stick together no matter what."

"What are you saying, Matt?" Nate asked, sticking his hands into his pockets, his head tilted as he studied him.

"I'm saying that we should re-think that whole business of sharing her." He drew in a deep breath. "If—and that's a big if—but if she does like us all, maybe we can convince her to stay with all of us."

"I think we need to get today out of the way," Nate murmured, his eyes on Matt's slightly rounded shoulders. "I think we need to listen to what Jonas makes of her, and then we need to figure out how we're going to help her. We've been fucking about here, thinking only of ourselves. We're about to drop a bomb on her that's going to shake everything she's ever known or believed in. Which one of us gets to fuck her is probably not what we ought to be concentrating on right now."

"It's not about fucking her, Nate!" Matt spat angrily.

"I know it's not, but I think we need to put her first. We promised to look after her, and we'd better make sure we hold up to that. We can't let her down now."

"And if she's something we're not expecting?" Jake asked. "If she's playing with us?"

"She's not." Matt shook his head, his hair falling into his eyes. He swept it sideways impatiently. "I know she's not."

"I agree," Nate said, nodding at Matt.

"But Nate's right, we have to think of her right now," Matt added. "She just…" Matt shoved a hand into his hair in frustration. "I just want to…"

"Look after her, be with her," Jake said quietly. "Touch her as much as possible."

"Hold her hand, talk to her," Josh added. "We just want to be around her, and when we're not, she's pretty much all we can think or talk about."

"Yeah," Matt agreed. "That's it."

"I think we all feel it," Nate said, staring down at his shoes. "Look, let's just shelve it for now and see how it plays out."

"Agreed," Josh and Jake said together.

"Then let's go change and get her," Matt said.

Lily stared at her reflection in the mirror that hung in the living room. She looked the same as she had the day before. Same long, dark, wavy hair that needed a good brushing more often than not, same pale face, same brown eyes, same dimples, same lips. Nothing had changed. And yet she was sure something had changed.

Nate told her she had hallucinated. Maybe she had. Maybe she hadn't. All she knew was that it felt real; extremely and frighteningly real. For those split seconds, the children had been there. She'd seen them both go under the water, had felt the frantic urgency to get them out.

But they hadn't been there. There were no children, no screams, other than her own.

She had been sure that she was going mad. Nate tried to calm her by telling her that he'd researched it and some epileptics also experienced hallucinations. The twins anchored her by sitting wrapped around her, and Matt soothed her with his gentle voice. They'd settled her, calmed her down enough to think rationally. But she couldn't ignore the fact that her seizures were changing again, and the lack of control she felt scared her. Nate said they were hallucinations, and a huge part of her wanted to believe that. But a smaller part, a darker, scared part, told her that they weren't hallucinations, but something else. Something that she wasn't sure she wanted to even acknowledge, let alone explore.

"Lily! Are you okay?" Her mother startled her from her thoughts.

"Yeah, just away with the fairies again," she said brightly. She started to brush her hair out, ready to braid. The last thing she wanted to do was scare her mother, so she would keep quiet.

Her mother took the brush and drew it gently through Lily's hair. "It's been years since I did this," she said affectionately. "Where has the time gone?" she murmured to herself. Lily watched as her mother tugged her hair into a French braid.

"Will you be okay today, Mum?"

"Yes, I'm going to town first. Then I want to make a start on the first oil, so I'll be out at the manor most of the day. If you want me, ring the manor, as I may not get reception on the mobile."

There was a knock at the door and Lily turned quickly. "That'll be the boys," she said, moving across to pick up her bag and push her feet into her canvas shoes.

"Be careful, Lily."

"They're perfectly safe, Mum."

"I meant be careful because of your seizures. I could have sworn you either had one last night, or were about to have one, you looked dreadful."

"All the fresh country air." Lily played it off, kissed her cheek, and went to open the door.

"All ready, Lily Flower?" Matt asked as soon as she had it open. He looked good in black jeans, a red shirt, and a black jacket over the top. The wide smile on his lips mirrored the happiness in his eyes.

"I am indeed. Bye, Mum," she called and went out, shutting the door, hearing her mother call back to her from the living room.

"How do you feel today?" he asked her, as he opened the gate for her.

"Much better than last night," she said. She climbed into the passenger side, saying hello to the others. "I want to apologise for last night."

"We told you not to worry about it." Nate reached forward to touch her shoulder. "Let's go and have some fun. Put your belt on, Lily May."

Lily nodded, pulling the belt around her. She was more than willing to push it all to the back of her mind. If she didn't actively think about it, it wasn't real.

Crocodiles

The abandoned quarry was in the middle of a bleak stretch of moorland that separated Trenance from the local town. The pool was surrounded on three sides with sheer faced rock, about twenty feet in height. The signs that it had been a quarry were clear to see. Piles of moss covered rocks lay forgotten, leftover from when they'd been cut out to get to the granite. The pool was shallow for a few feet and then dropped abruptly away into deep water. It was peaceful, the water completely still, like obsidian, not even the slight breeze making it ripple.

"Are there any fish in there?" Lily asked, turning to see everyone setting their backpacks on the rocks.

"I've never seen any," Nate said. "But it's perfectly safe, nothing will nibble at you."

"Nothing?" Josh sniggered as he sat on the rock and took off his boots. She narrowed her eyes at him.

"Is there anything in there?" she asked him. He looked up at her and snapped his teeth together repeatedly before smirking at her.

"There's nothing that will hurt you," Matt said. "Ignore him."

"It would be just my luck that someone released a crocodile in there last night." She crossed back over to her bag.

"Crocodile?" Jake looked at her, grinning. "You have a wild imagination. Why would someone release a crocodile in there?"

"Well, you know, sometimes people get these exotic pets that grow too big, or they can't handle them anymore, and then they release them into the wild."

"I think you can relax; no one in Trenance has had a pet crocodile recently," Nate said quietly, humour colouring his voice.

"Well, you can go in first." She grinned at him.

He straightened and tilted his head, arching one eyebrow at her. "Why, thank you, Lily May. It means a lot that you're happy to sacrifice me to make sure it's safe for you."

She shrugged at him, still grinning. "You'd be my hero." She undid her jacket.

"We can all be your heroes," Matt spoke up quickly.

"Speaking of heroes, this is the smallest wetsuit we have. It's a few years old, but perfectly good still." Josh stood up and took a black wetsuit from his backpack. "They can be a pig to get on, so we'll help you."

Lily's fingers hesitated on the edges of her hooded jumper. It suddenly occurred to her that she was going to be in nothing but a swimsuit with them; nerves made her fingers hesitate. She looked at Nate stripping off his top, completely oblivious that he was now bare chested in front of her. He wasn't overly muscled, but she could see that his stomach was flat with just a hint of a six pack; a dark line of hair trailed from underneath his belly button down into his jeans. She coloured up and looked away hastily, just to see Matt pulling his jeans off. He had board shorts on underneath, and he was just as gorgeous as Nate. She made a small noise and hastily pulled the top over her head, as she turned her back to them. She drew her jeans off and then sat on the rock, bringing her knees to her chest to keep warm. She was careful to not look at the twins who were now stripping off. They weren't the first boys she'd ever seen that were gorgeous. Some of the boys in her tutor group were good looking, and Jimmy had been good looking as well. But there was something different with these boys. She hadn't felt so aware of a boy before as she did them.

"You'll freeze!" Josh exclaimed. They came over with the wetsuit.

"How do we want to do this, Joshua?" Jake was still in just his shorts. They hung low on his hips, and she was aware that he was just as gorgeous as Nate and Matt. Josh came into her line of vision and her mouth went dry.

"Turn it inside out, Jacob. It'll be a lot easier that way."

She watched as between them they turned the wetsuit inside out, glad that it gave her something to look at instead of drooling over them.

Matt and Nate came over, their wetsuits on and battered trainers on their feet. Josh caught her eye by going to his knees on the grass at her feet.

"We're going to roll it onto you, okay?" He looked up at her through his fringe. Her breath caught in her throat and she nodded at him, unable to say anything coherent.

Jake knelt next to him and she felt them slide her tennis shoes off before working the wetsuit over her feet. Fingers ran over the bottoms of her feet as they eased the fabric on. She let out a squeak and scrambled backwards, trying to get away from the tickling of their fingers.

"Lily is ticklish," Jake announced with glee and grabbed her foot, the wetsuit forgotten. He ran his fingertips up and down her sole as he watched her, a wicked grin tugged his lips.

"No!" She tried to kick out at him but his hold was tight. Josh caught her other foot, and she collapsed back wriggling as she squealed with laughter. She fought to get away, but they were stronger than she was.

"We thought someone was drowning!"

Her feet were instantly released, and she was pulled upright between them. Disorientated by the quickness she found herself surrounded by the four of them, blocking her from whomever was coming down the path.

"Ben. Hey, man," Nate called out, and she felt them relax slightly. Josh and Jake turned back to her, and bending, they began to roll the wetsuit up her legs quickly. It was a tight fit and they hesitated when they reached mid-thigh. She gripped the edges and tugged it up over her hips, wiggling to get it into place.

"Hey, you guys going in?" She saw three boys go past her and leave their bags near where she and the boys had left their own. "Who's that? Oh, it's the new chick."

Lily looked over Josh's shoulder as she started to roll the stiff material up her arms. Nate and Matt moved over to talk to them as Josh helped her tug it up towards her neck. She was turned, and the zip was pulled upwards. It was too tight from her waist up, but it would do. She wriggled slightly, trying to get used to the restrictiveness of it.

Nate and Matt came back over, and she watched as the other boys climbed up to where there was a ledge that jutted out slightly over the pool. They shouted as they took a running jump into the water and then started to muck around together. Josh and Jake struggled into their wetsuits.

"Damn, I was hoping it would just be us," Nate muttered as he did up Matt's wetsuit and then turned to let Matt help him with his own. Neither of them used the long cords attached to zips, instead, they just relied on each other.

"They might go soon," Josh said. "They're just in shorts and t-shirts, it'll be too cold to stay in there like that. Put your shoes back on, Lily."

Lily stuffed her feet back into her shoes, tugging at the neck of the suit. She looked up and saw all of them looking at her, but their eyes seemed to be stuck at chest level.

"What?" All four of them looked up quickly, and she realised with a blush that she'd caught them checking out her chest.

"Yeah. So... yeah." Matt had the grace to blush as he ran a hand through his hair, but the other three just smirked at her.

"Lily, it's hard not to," Josh said, and reached forwards to gently tug on her braid. "You're gorgeous." He winked at her and gripped her hand. "Try not to swallow too much water. Hold your breath, and don't let go."

"Don't throw me in!" She tugged her hand free and backed up from them. Nate put his hand on her lower back, his thumb rotating circles that she felt even through the thick fabric.

"We won't throw you in, but if you try to wade in, you won't make it. You'll be turning around before you even get to your knees," Nate said. "It's colder than river or sea water."

"Okay, but don't push me." She crossed her arms across her chest, but it just served to push her bust out even more, and she was once again aware of their eyes dropping. She rolled her eyes and reached forward to slap Josh on the chest. He gave her a wounded look that quickly turned into a smirk.

"We'll never push you, Lily Flower. Be warned though, it's freezing. No one I know wades in. We all jump from there." Matt pointed to the rock that the boys had jumped from. The water was inky black there, and she knew it was deep.

"Can you go in first, please?" she asked.

"In case the crocodile is feeling hungry?" Nate asked, and chuckling he took his contact lenses out and put them into a special case in his bag. They went across to the rocks, and she climbed up behind Nate.

Nate took a running jump and went down into the black water, causing a huge splash. She watched and saw him surface a couple of feet away. He slicked his hair back, treading water as he grinned up at them.

"It's freezing," he yelled. "Come on down, Lily May!"

Lily looked at Matt. A rush of adrenaline flowed through her, and she grinned. She moved right to the edge of the rock, ready to jump but was tugged back abruptly by Matt.

"Don't jump straight down, you could hit the side of the rocks. Take a running jump and aim to get at least three feet from the edge. It's safer."

She looked up at him. He was watching her, a small smile played around his lips, his eyes warm. She reached out and pushed a strand of hair out of his eyes, his smile softened, and a warm feeling filled her. They really looked after her, and she could get used to that.

He leant forward and pressed his lips to hers gently, making her heart flip in her chest. He pulled back from her and with a smile he ran off the edge, yelling as he went down, hugging his knees to his chest.

"Want us to wait for you, or go on?" Josh spoke up; his voice was quiet with an edge that she hadn't heard before. She turned to look at them, but they weren't looking at her. They were both looking to where Matt was swimming towards Nate. She saw Ben start to climb back up to jump in again; they'd have to move to make room for him.

"Can we jump in together, or is it too dangerous?" she asked, holding out her hands to them. Jake looked up at her, and she saw something reflected in his eyes that she didn't quite get. They came forward and took hold of her hands.

"On three, run and jump," Josh said, his voice calm. Lily nodded, nerves and excitement making her heart beat faster. They clutched her hands tightly. Josh counted, and then she was running and jumping with them.

They'd warned her it was cold, but nothing could have prepared her for just how cold it was. She hit the water feet first and plunged downwards. Her breath ripped from her as the water closed over her head. She could feel them holding her hands tightly as the downward momentum kept them going. It felt like she'd jumped into a pit of freezing needles that were tearing at her despite the wetsuit. She kept her mouth shut and her eyes open, but she could see nothing past the eruption of bubbles and black water. Fear slammed through her, and she ripped her hands free from theirs, kicking and trying to work herself back up. She broke through the surface, taking a huge lungful of air as she treaded water. She pushed her hair free from her face, glad that she had braided it. Josh and Jake broke through the surface beside her, gulping in air.

"It's freezing," she cried out, laughing with the exhilaration that filled her now that the fear was gone.

"Yeah!" Jake laughed and swam towards her. He gripped her around the waist and started to tug her towards the others. "C'mon, you don't want to be underneath them when they jump."

The other boys were waiting for a clear area before they jumped, and she forced herself to swim alongside the twins. As she swam, she began to get used to the coldness, and she realised that to be able to stay in she'd have to keep moving. She made it to where the others were and treaded water again, her teeth chattering as she looked back at the boys ready to jump. They were all gathered at the edge, hugging themselves against the cold as they talked.

"Need to keep moving," she stuttered and began to swim towards the shallow area.

"Crocodile!" She heard Matt yell, and she looked back to see him swimming towards her quickly. He caught her around her waist, and she was lifted and thrown a little way forward, Matt's laughter in her ears. She turned, spluttering, and flicked water at him. He made to dive towards her again, and she gave a squeal of laughter and set off for the shallow bit. When she could finally put her feet down, she turned and looked back. Matt snapped his teeth at her, looming over her. Josh slid his arm around her and snapped his teeth as well.

"Going to eat you all up," Jake said, making claws with his hands. He caught her around the waist, and she cried out with laughter, trying to move away from them. Jake just laughed evilly and lifted her right up into the air. Her hands went to his shoulders instinctively, laughing as she looked down at him.

"I'm a croc hunter. I'll save you," Nate called out. Jake launched her through the air to Nate. He caught her close, his arms around her. She was breathless with laughter, her hands on his shoulders.

"What do I get for saving you?" he asked. His eyes held hers, and her laughter died on her lips. She wondered what he'd do if she kissed him.

"Coming through!"

Nate let her go; the moment was broken, and Lily felt a shiver of disappointment. Nate moved them both to one side as the boys pushed through the water beside them. They all eyed Lily, smirks on their faces as they passed her. She avoided eye contact with all of them and turned away.

"Let's race," Matt spoke up. "Those kids are happy to just jump in; if we stick to the left side, we can race and not get in their way."

"I'm not a great swimmer," Lily said. "I won't beat you."

"You don't have to beat us, Lily May. Just try and keep up."

"And if I can't even keep up?" she asked, hugging her arms around her, her teeth chattering again.

"It doesn't matter, we aren't going anywhere. We'll wait for you, Lily Pad," Jake said. "We'll give you a head start if you want."

She grinned and stepped forwards slightly. "I'll take you up on that, I really don't swim well."

"Don't you go often?" asked Matt. He was poking at his ear, head tilted to the side, to get the water out.

"Not really. Never get the chance."

"Off you go then, Lily Flower. We'll give you a thirty second start."

She grinned and struck out in a crawl. She made good progress, but she didn't have the power they did and they quickly caught up with her. They kept pace with her until about halfway to the other side. Then they powered ahead, and she knew they were racing each other now. She changed to the breast stroke, unable to keep up the crawl. She could see them clinging to the rocks, calling encouragement to her to keep going, and it spurred her on.

Suddenly, something grabbed her foot and she went under, terror slamming through her. Images of crocodiles went through her head. Hands gripped her painfully, and she was pulled back through the water and then lifted high in the air. She was thrown forwards and landed awkwardly in the water. She fought to get to the surface, coughing and choking on the water, and then she was being grabbed and lifted again. She fought him, struggling in his hold, trying to get him to put her down, but he hoisted her easily out of the water, and she felt herself being thrown again. She went under, and terror filled every pore. They weren't letting her get her breath and she was inhaling too much water. She was going to drown. Hands pulled at her arms, and she struck out again, not able to take anymore.

"Lily!"

She recognised Matt's voice and stopped struggling. He hooked his hands under her armpits and began towing her back to the shallows. He dragged her out onto the bank, and she went to her hands and knees, coughing up the water she'd swallowed. Relief flowed through her as he banged her back firmly, helping her to bring the water up. He'd saved her.

"It's okay. You're okay." Matt's voice was gentle in her ear, his head close to hers. She nodded, still coughing. She was safe. He had kept her safe, but it had been scary. The feeling of the water closing over her, unable to catch her breath, wasn't something she wanted to repeat ever again.

"What the fucking hell did you think you were doing?" She heard one of the twins shouting angrily.

"We were just playing with her. You were chucking her about just a minute ago."

"You almost drowned her, asshole!" She heard a scuffle as she turned to slump down onto the grass. She could see Josh, Jake, and Nate facing off against the three other boys. She tried to get her breath, shivers wracking through her as the cold seeped through the material of the suit. Matt draped a towel around her and then pulled her onto his lap, holding her tightly. She cuddled into him, his chin on the top of her head. She realised it was an intimate hold, but she couldn't move even if she wanted to, and she didn't want to. She felt safe in his arms. Safe and comfortable.

She saw Josh reach forward and shove one of the boys in the chest. He went backwards, but Josh just followed him, his finger poking his chest as he growled at him, too low for Lily to hear.

"Don't let them fight." Her voice was a little husky from coughing.

"They won't fight," Matt said.

The boys stalked towards her, angry snarls on their faces. They hesitated as they looked down at her, and she saw regret in their faces. They hadn't been trying to drown her, they were just being stupid.

"We didn't mean to hurt you, we were just having fun."

She nodded, looking up at them. "It's okay," she whispered.

"No, it's not," Matt contradicted her. "You nearly drowned her."

"We're fucking sorry, alright?" They walked away, muttering as they grabbed their bags and disappeared over the rise of the path.

"Damn, that was not supposed to happen," Josh grunted and sat down beside them. "Are you okay, Lily?"

"I'm fine. I just couldn't get my breath, but I'm fine now, honest. Thanks for rescuing me." She patted Matt on the arm that encircled her waist.

"And thank you for stopping them," she said to the others.

Josh plucked her out of Matt's arms and onto his lap. Jake settled beside him, and she was moved till she was sitting half on Jake's and half on Josh's laps as they held her between them tightly. Their arms were wrapped right around her, and she stiffened, unsure why they were doing it. Lips brushed over the top of her head, and it no longer mattered why they were doing it. She melted into their hold with a sigh. She was attracted to all of them, but she realised it was more than that. It went deeper than mere attraction; she felt the same connection with all of them. Being held by them wasn't awkward, it didn't make her nervous. This was right, this was where she was supposed to be. With them.

"We need to make a move, get dressed again before we get too cold." Nate's voice had the twins moving back. She started to shift forwards to get up, but hands slid under her arms and she was lifted to her feet, Nate's face inches from hers.

"Are you sure you're okay?" he murmured, his blue eyes searching her face. She saw a smattering of tiny freckles over his nose that weren't noticeable at a distance. His eyes caught hers, and she nodded at him, not sure she could trust her voice this close to him. He tilted his head and pulled her into him tightly, his arms wrapped around her, his face going into her neck. She felt his lips brush the skin under her ear, and she shuddered violently, but he just held her tighter and something settled deep inside her. He set her back from him and turned to the twins.

"Go and make sure those losers have gone so Lily can change," he ordered. They jumped to their feet and headed up the path. Nate looked back at Lily and reached out to touch the end of her nose. "You need to get dressed before you catch a chill. We'll turn our backs, okay?"

"Get dressed, Lily Flower," Matt said softly as he moved past her. "We'll take you to see a friend of ours in the village; he'll get us warmed up with coffee."

"I don't want to impose on him," Lily spoke up, crossing to her bag.

"We won't be. He's been putting up with us just dropping in at any time for years. He was our teacher in primary; he's a great man, you'll love him."

"Whose towel have I got?" she asked, seeing her own in the bag.

"We brought extra, just in case," Nate spoke up, pulling a towel from his bag. The twins came back, talking together quietly but stopped before she could hear what they were saying.

"They've gone," Jake said, and came over to Lily. He stepped up behind her and drew the zip down on her wetsuit, and then moved away again.

Lily saw them turn their backs as they concentrated on getting out of their own wetsuits. She tried to work it off but it was tough, and she couldn't get a grip on it to get it down her arms. No matter how hard she tugged, she couldn't get it to move.

She admitted defeat and called out to them. "Can I have a hand, please?" Matt came towards her and started to unpeel her from the suit, making her laugh.

"It's like peeling an onion." She laughed as the wetsuit landed around her ankles with a wet plop. Matt crouched down and touched her foot. She balanced herself with one hand on his shoulder and lifted her leg. He tugged it off and then repeated the process with her other foot. He stood up and set his nose against her cheek and sniffed deeply.

"You smell too good to be an onion." He chuckled and turned back to carry on dressing. She lifted her towel and wrapped it around herself, suddenly conscious that she was going to be stripping out of her swimsuit with them there. They kept their backs to her as they peeled off their own wetsuits. Nate's board shorts pulled down with the suit and she got an eyeful of his firm butt that made her breath catch in her throat. She turned away. Part of her wanted to watch, but she knew that was wrong on all sorts of levels, not least of all by betraying a privacy they were extending to her. She stayed under the towel and wriggled out of her swimsuit. She dried as best as she could and then shimmied into her clothes, still under the towel. She dropped the towel as she dragged her jeans up her hips. She did them up and turned to face them. They were finished before her, but they were still facing away, talking quietly together.

"I'm ready." She pushed her feet into the dry pair of trainers she'd brought with her.

"When you get back tonight," Josh said, coming towards her with Jake beside him. "Wash the wetsuit off, and then hang it to dry outside."

"I'll give it back to you on Monday."

He shook his head. "We gave it to you. It's yours now, Lily Pad."

"Thank you." She leant forward and kissed Josh on the cheek and then turned to Jake. Just as she drew close, he turned his head and his lips brushed hers deliberately. She backed up quickly, turning to get her backpack, feeling flustered again. He'd kissed her.

Matt had kissed her. She didn't think friends kissed like that. But they hadn't said anything, so it could be nothing more than friendship to them. She could see herself dating them, but she couldn't see herself being able to choose one over the other. And that would be a problem if they liked her too.

She couldn't have them all; but she couldn't, wouldn't, choose just one.

Other than kisses, and if she was honest they weren't more than a peck, none of them gave any indication they wanted to date her. She was reading into things that just weren't there. She was probably having internal debates over not falling for them, and all they wanted was another friend. She had to stop her heart from ruling her head. They were just friends. Good friends, and that was all they would stay.

The Seer

One of the advantages of being constantly on the move was that Lily learnt how to interact with people she didn't know. She could put a smile on her face and be easy going while hiding all sorts of emotions, like nerves and shyness.

Jonas Rutledge was like no one she had ever met before, though. Whether it was because she knew he was a teacher and she never interacted with them outside of classrooms, or whether it was because he had clear blue eyes that she was certain could see right into her soul, she didn't know. Whatever it was, she didn't feel completely comfortable with him. She felt as if she had to be on her best behaviour; her back ramrod straight as she perched on the edge of the sofa, a mug of coffee clutched in her hands.

Her eyes darted around the room, trying not to be too nosey, but fascinated with what she could get quick glimpses of. The boys, however, had no such worries as they sprawled around his living room as if it was their own house. Matt sat beside her while Nate sat at a desk under the window, spinning the globe that sat on top of the desk. The twins were slumped on the other sofa staring at her, which made her feel even more uncomfortable. Josh had a cat, Mysty, curled up on his lap, and he was scratching it behind the ear.

The room was crammed full of books. There were books on shelves, desks, and in piles on the floor. Lily had never seen so many books outside of a library, and it made her hands itch to see what he had. A large map of the ancient world was the only framed picture in the room that she could see at a quick glance. It hung above the fireplace. The mantelpiece was crammed with wooden carvings and a clock that was so old that it looked as if it had been made at the same time as the house. She could hear it ticking from where she sat. She let herself look at it for a few minutes and saw it was one that had the sun and the moon appearing on the face, depending on the time of day. Either side of the fireplace were wall fittings that looked like gas lights but had probably been converted to electric.

"Where did you move from, Lily?" Jonas sat in the armchair by the fire. His fingers steepled under his nose as he watched her, elbows resting on the arms of the chair.

"Brighton, I mean Portsmouth. No, well, Brighton then Portsmouth," she said, nerves making her babble. She coloured up and hastily looked down at her coffee mug. He was weighing her in the balance, and she could see that the jury was still out on his decision.

"Lily moved to Portsmouth at the beginning of the summer from Brighton, but then came here just over a week ago." Nate spoke up, and she nodded, thankful for his help clarifying. She took a sip of her coffee and spilled some down her chin. She wiped it away hastily, her cheeks bright red with embarrassment. She was messing this up big time, but every sense she had was on high alert. It wasn't as if he could give her detention or give her fifty lines. She just knew that he was obviously important to the boys, and she didn't want to let them down.

"Matthew was explaining you have epilepsy." Jonas stretched his legs out in front of him. "That must be quite tiring." There was no hint of pity in his voice, and for that she was glad.

Lily shrugged, her eyes on the pattern of her mug. "I've always had it, so I don't really think about it," she admitted.

"Still, it would be restrictive," he said and suddenly got to his feet. It startled her, and she jumped, spilling some of the coffee onto her jeans. She hastily wiped at it, apologising as she did. He came over and took the mug from her and then gripped her hand. She made a strangled noise in the back of her throat at his unexpected actions.

"Look at me." His voice was deep, commanding, and she found herself obeying him.

Her eyes met his, and it was instant. She could feel herself falling, her eyes rolling back into her head. Something was being pushed into her mind. She could hear voices, see flashes of images that didn't make sense. She wasn't in his house anymore. A schoolyard. A bird that was fluttering around on the ground. A much younger Matt picking it up. The bird flying away. The images raced through her mind quickly, like cartoons on a TV.

Her hand was released, and she slumped back heavily. The images cleared; she was in his living room, not a schoolyard. A searing pain made her grip her head, crying out. Fear filled her as she struggled to comprehend what had happened. Did he cause that? Did she have another fit? She couldn't think through the pure agony in her head.

"Lily, Lily." Matt's voice in her ear had her struggling to get away from him. She didn't understand what was happening to her. Fear morphed into terror as she felt her hands being pulled from her head.

"No, get off me!" she cried out, the pain making tears course down her face. She was dying. Whatever he'd done, she was dying. She heard Nate order Matt to do something, and then a hand was placed over her forehead. It felt cool against her heated skin, and then as quickly as it came, the pain left her. Matt grunted, and she looked towards him in panic, her hands clutching the sofa she was sitting on. Blood was pouring from Matt's nose. Josh, or was it Jake, stuffed a cloth under his nose, and then all four of them were surrounding her, hands on her knees, back, and shoulders.

"What the fuck did you do to her?" Nate demanded, rounding on Jonas angrily. Matt had the cloth stuffed against his nose with one hand, his other on her shoulder, but they were all looking at Jonas. Lily looked over at him, the fear growing in her mind. He was sitting back in his chair, fingers once again steepled under his nose as he studied her. She couldn't bring herself to meet his eyes. She needed to get out of there; she started to push herself up, trying to get through the boys. She didn't know what was going on, but she knew she was in danger. There was something hugely wrong, and her fear was making her sweat.

"I wanted to see one of her fits," he said calmly. "Lily, I can tell you one thing, that was not an epileptic seizure. You do not have epilepsy."

"What?" His words, completely unexpected, stopped her in her tracks. She looked at him, her eyes going no higher than the top button of his polo shirt. "What are you talking about?" Fear crouched in her mind, threatening to overwhelm her.

"You saw things, didn't you," he said calmly. "You saw Matthew as a boy, in a schoolyard. And a bird, didn't you?"

She gasped. How had he known that? She looked at his eyes, but he was no longer looking at her, but into the dead ashes of the fireplace.

"Lily, we need to talk to you," Nate said. "But we need you to keep an open mind, and we need you to promise that you won't repeat what we talk about here."

"What?" She was repeating herself, she knew it. But nothing was making sense, and a feeling of impending doom was hovering over her. She wasn't sure she wanted to hear what they were going to say. She shook her head in denial, but Josh and Jake caught her hands in theirs and crept closer till they were pressed against her knees. She couldn't take her eyes away from Jonas staring into the fireplace. He was lost in thought, a frown tugging his eyebrows together. She didn't understand what was happening to her. She felt as if she'd been cast adrift at sea with nothing to hold onto and she was terrified she was going to drown.

"Please, Lily, listen," Josh begged her.

She dragged her eyes away from Jonas to meet his gaze.

"What did he do to me?" she demanded. There had to be a logical explanation to all of this, she was just missing it in her panic.

She forced herself to calm down, to think rationally, refusing to give into the confused terror.

"We don't think you get epileptic fits, Lily," Nate said quietly. "That first time we met you, you fitted because you touched Matt."

"I don't... no!" She shook her head, trying to process what he was saying. Why was he saying that? "I have epilepsy. I've been to enough doctors over the years and had enough CAT scans to know what I have." Confusion filled her as she looked back at Matt. His nose had stopped bleeding, and he was dabbing at it, his eyes on her. "What did you do to me?" she demanded.

"I took away your headache," he said quietly. "It's not the first time I've done it. I made you sleep it off when you left last night."

"What do you mean you took away... no, no, that's not possible." She shook her head, trying to push herself back away from them. "Why are you doing this?"

"Because we care about you, Lily May. You're one of us."

One of them? Was this some kind of weird initiation thing they had going on? Was it some horrendous joke, or a test, or some crazy thing she had to do to be part of their group?

"One of you? What are you talking about?"

"We're Fae, and you are a Seer," Matt said quietly.

"You're...." She stopped and stared at him. She studied his eyes, trying to find the light of humour in them, because they were obviously playing a trick on her. And a rotten one at that.

"Your fits aren't epilepsy, they're visions. You've been having visions," Josh said. She looked down to where he was sitting back on his heels next to Jake. They were shoulder to shoulder again, hair hung into their eyes; eyes which were squinted in concern.

"Did he put something into your coffee?" she whispered, looking at Nate. "Do you feel strange? Slightly light headed?" It was the only explanation she could come up with, that they were currently high on something. But that didn't explain what Jonas had done to her, where the images and sounds had come from, nor the blinding headache which Matt appeared to have taken away with a touch of his hand, leaving him with a bloody nose. Unless her own coffee was also spiked, and this was some dreadful trip. Horror filled her as she looked over to where her mug sat on the coffee table.

"We're not high, Lily May," Nate said. "We're not drugged, and neither are you. We're Fae. Fairies if you must call us that, although I really don't—"

"Fairies?" She cut him off. That was the last thing she expected him to say. "Fairies as in Tinkerbell, and wings, and pixie dust?" she asked in derision. Did they really think she was an idiot?

"No, not like Tinkerbell. Tinkerbell was a pixie, not a fairy, and she wasn't real either! Just listen to us!" Nate bit out, irritation in his voice, and it sparked her own anger.

"Okay, show me your wings then!" It was clear they were messing with her and betrayal shot through her, closely teamed with anger.

"We don't have wings," Jake said, his hand on her knee still.

"Of course you don't! Because that's not possible, is it?" She shoved their hands from her knees and got up, pulling herself free from Matt and Nate.

"You're thinking of story books," Matt said quickly. "You need to forget everything you've read or heard over the years, Lily."

"I need to forget…" She shook her head and looked down at them. "You think I'm stupid, don't you? You're having a laugh at my expense. Oh, look, it's the new girl who has fits, let's mess with her mind. Make her think we like her, and then play a joke on her."

She shoved past Josh and Jake to get to the door. "I've met people like you before, idiots that think it's funny I have fits. Idiots that reckon it's cool to try and make me fit just so they can get a kick out of watching me twitch about like a... like a...." Words failed her as anger crashed around her, leaving her devastated and hurting. She hurt so badly it felt like her heart was being ripped from her chest. Tears spilled from her eyes. "You made me care about you! You made me like you more than I should!" She saw them get to their feet, desperation on their faces, but she wasn't going to be caught like that again.

"Lily, we're telling you the truth! We know it's hard to understand. Nate! Show her!" Matt nudged Nate's shoulder urgently.

"Lily May, look!" Nate held up his hands, palms upwards, and she saw two blue flames dancing on them. For a second it threw her, made her gasp as she stumbled back slightly. But then she remembered the street entertainers she'd seen in London. They could do things that defied gravity. Sleight of hand made all sorts of things look possible. She shook her head angrily, her eyes locking with Nate's.

"You should perform on the streets of London," she said, wiping away the tears that were still dripping down her face. "You'd be ten a penny though."

"I'm not performing, come and touch it, Lily May," he commanded her. His head was tilted slightly to the left, his eyes were even bluer, a shine to them that almost had her stepping forward.

"No, I won't let you hurt me anymore," she cried out. She turned and ran from the room, her heart beating painfully in her chest. It felt like her whole world was collapsing around her. She couldn't bear the pain of their betrayal. They'd been playing with her this whole time. Playing with her feelings and her emotions. They'd seen her vulnerability and used it against her. They'd made her want so much more from them, and it made her hate herself. She'd been so needy, so blind, so caught up by how they looked after her, how they made her feel when they touched her, that she'd missed their motives. She had been played for a fool.

She slammed the front door behind her and ran down the road, not caring where she went, blinded by pain and tears. She finally came to a stop when she was unable to run anymore, pain ripped through her sides as she bent, hands on her knees, her breathing heavy.

She had made a fool of herself. It was her fault she'd left herself wide open. She should never have let them get so close to her. Why would they do something like that, though? She'd had jokes played on her before, been bullied as the new girl, but never had it made her hurt as much as they had.

As practical jokes went, it was the most far-fetched. Fae, fairies, magic, what sort of idiot did they think she was?

"Lily? Lily!" She heard her name being called, and for a heart stopping second she thought it was them. But when she looked up it was the man from the optician's. He was on the other side of the busy road, getting out of his car. Concern was clear to see on his face.

"Are you okay? What's wrong?" He shut his door, and then checking both ways he dodged the passing cars to run across to her. He wore a black suit with a white shirt and a red tie, making him look professional.

"Lily, I saw you running down the street as if the hounds of hell were on your heels. Are you in trouble? Is someone chasing you?" He didn't touch her, but he did look her up and down, as if assessing her for damage.

"No, I'm fine… I'm…" She realised she didn't know where she was, or how to get back to the village. Jonas lived in the town and with a sinking feeling she realised she'd left her backpack at his house, along with her phone and money. She was completely lost with nowhere to turn, except back to them.

"You're not fine, Lily." He stepped forward and brought a handkerchief from his pocket for her. "Let me take you home. I'm on my way back to Trenance anyway."

Lily took it from him with a quiet thanks. She didn't know what to do. She didn't want to go back there and get her bag. She couldn't face them so soon. She wasn't sure she'd ever be able to face them again.

"Have you been swimming?" he asked, pushing his hands into his trouser pockets. His head was slightly tilted, and it reminded her of Nate. Nate with his parlour tricks.

"Yes, I, um, earlier in the quarry." She touched her still wet hair with a shaky hand. It seemed like years ago. They'd looked after her then. How could they look after her so well and then do something so cruel? Fresh tears started to roll down her face, and he grunted. She buried her face in his handkerchief.

"Lily, you have no coat on and no bag with you. Are you in trouble? Is someone trying to hurt you?"

"No. I..." Lily looked up to see him pulling out his phone.

"Do you need me to call the police, Lily?"

"No!" His words shocked her into trying to pull herself together. She was worrying him and that wasn't fair. "No, I'm fine. Honestly, I just had an argument with someone, and now I'm lost."

"Let me take you home," he said gently. He held his hands towards her, palms up as if telling her he wouldn't hurt her. She took a deep breath and looked back the way she'd come, but there was no sign of them, and it just made the pain even worse. She looked back at him and nodded once. His face broke into a gentle smile, and he turned sideways, indicating his car with his hand outstretched.

"I'm Drew, by the way." He took her elbow in a gentle touch, and then checked both ways before drawing her across the road quickly. He took her around to the passenger side and held the door open for her.

She sank into the comfortable seat, clicking her seat belt into place. He shut the door, and it sank in what she had done. She had just done what sensible people never did. Get into a stranger's car.

He ran around the back of the car and slid into his seat. Her hand went to the clip, but he shut his door and pulled out into the road quickly.

"I know you're Lily," he said calmly. He hadn't put his own belt on, but she said nothing, just stared straight ahead, her heartbeat going a million beats a minute.

"I heard your mum call you Lily last night," he said conversationally as he manoeuvred the car into the outside lane for the roundabout coming up. She searched for road signs and saw that they were headed for Trenance; a measure of relief filled her. "I didn't want to call out to you in case I scared you," he said softly.

His words sank in, and she looked at him, his handkerchief still bunched in her fingers. "Was that you last night smoking?" she asked, feeling more secure.

He winced and nodded. "Yes, I'm renting the place and there's a no smoking policy inside. It's a terrible habit, one I should kick really. I hope you don't smoke, Lily."

She shook her head, her nerves receding the closer they got to the village. She was feeling wrung out, exhausted, she just wanted to go home. To lick her wounds in peace, to kick herself for believing in a friendship that never was.

"Good for you. Don't start," he said.

"Are you looking to move here then?" she asked, trying to keep her voice level. She didn't want him asking questions about what had happened. He didn't need to know how much of an idiot she'd been.

"No. I'm a history professor on a sabbatical. I'm researching the Cornish history of smuggling for a book. Trenance is the next village on my trip around the coastline. There are caves close by that smugglers used extensively along the shoreline."

"Matt was telling—" She ground to a halt when it just dragged her mind back to Matt and the others.

"Matt?" he asked quietly. "Is that who you were arguing with? Your boyfriend?"

"He's not my boyfriend," she replied, turning her head to stare out of the windows. The houses were getting further and further apart as they headed out of town.

"Then he's a fool to not have snapped you up." He spoke lightly, but it sent a ripple of tension down her spine.

"I don't know him very well," she murmured. "We only moved in recently." Something she should be reminding herself of more frequently.

"Ah, so you're not a native." He chuckled, his eyes on the rear-view mirror. She turned to look behind her, but the winding country lanes made it difficult to see if anyone was behind them. But she had no reason to think they'd follow her. "Where are you from?" he asked, bringing her attention back to him.

"I was born in Glastonbury, but I've moved around a lot."

"Ah, Glastonbury: home to the Isle of Avalon, Chalice Hill and the Chalice Well, Druids and New Age mysticism. Very famous," he murmured happily, as if it was a place he knew well and loved.

"You forgot the festival." As far as Lily knew that was what Glastonbury was most famous for.

"You're talking to a historian," he said with a snort. "I'm a ninety-year-old trapped in the body of a thirty something. I'm old before my time and history gets me more excited than a sweaty, heaving, pot fuelled weekend ever could. And, yes, I do realise how sad that sounds." He chuckled. "Have you ever been to one of the festivals?"

"I have epilepsy." She rubbed her eyes. She was completely drained, her emotions all over the place still and it made her tongue loose. "I don't have photosensitive epilepsy, but Mum thinks it best I don't go anywhere that might cause a seizure."

"Really?" He looked at her sideways quickly, before concentrating on the road again. "That's a shame," he murmured. "Is that why you were arguing with your friend? Does he not understand?"

Lily kept quiet and just shrugged. The heating was on a low setting, and it was beginning to make her feel sleepy. She could smell sandalwood and something else; it reminded her of health food stores. She closed her eyes, feeling more peaceful.

"What's troubling you, Lily?" His voice was low and soothing to her stressed mind.

"Just some people aren't what they seem, I guess," she murmured and stifled a yawn, her eyes watching the passing hedges without really seeing them.

"Yeah, that's the truth." He slowed right down as they came up behind a tractor. It was taking up most of the road, and there were no places to pass just yet.

"Have you ever seen anything that you didn't think was possible? Been expected to accept something that seemed impossible?" The words spilled from her, and she winced, regretting it the moment she'd spoken.

"Well, yeah, sure, I guess," he said slowly. They stopped as the tractor came to a halt, the driver jumped out to open a gate leading into a field. He hailed Drew, thanking him for his patience, and Drew lifted his hand in acknowledgement. "I travelled a lot as a child." He kept his eyes on her as he waited. "I saw a lot of things that had no seeming plausibility to it, but they were real. I've seen monks walk on sand without leaving any footprints, I've seen people charm poisonous snakes. I've watched people pass through flames and remain unhurt. Watched people climb ropes suspended on nothing, defying gravity. I even tried that myself, but the rope was just a rope when I touched it."

"And they were really doing it?" she asked skeptically. She sat up straighter and turned slightly in her seat to face him.

"Yes, well, why wouldn't they?" he asked her, his eyes holding hers. "Sometimes things seem impossible because we don't understand it, but it doesn't stop it from being true, or real." The tractor honked in thanks, and he looked back at the road, pulling forward again. "Take black holes in space; they're not understood completely, but they're still there."

"What about magic? Do you believe in magic?" she asked him. She expected him to laugh at her, to shake his head and say no. She didn't expect him to shrug.

"I'm a historian. You'd be surprised how many things that seem to be myth and legend, are rooted in fact," he said quietly. He slowed down again as they neared the outskirts of the village. "Some of the things I saw smacked of magic. I wouldn't discount magic just because it doesn't seem possible. Lots of things seem impossible until someone does them. The Wright brothers built and flew the first heavier than air aeroplane, but I doubted they would have believed the stealth bomber to be possible. And if you'd have told a Viking that one-day man would walk on the moon, he would have laughed in your face. But both of those things are now possible because we have a better understanding. Maybe magic is out there, but we just don't understand it."

She knew what he was saying; could even see the logic in it. But magic? Fairies? She closed her eyes, another headache brewing behind them. Were they telling her the truth? No, surely it was impossible, this was the real world, not a story book.

"Maybe we're looking at things wrong," he said quietly as he pulled the car to a stop outside the cottages. "If you said to Orville or Wilbur Wright that we'd put a supersonic jet into the air, they'd be thinking in terms of their own invention shape, their own limitations in engine design. Maybe we look at magic and think of spells, cauldrons, wands. Women dressed in black robes with green faces and cats balancing on the end of broomsticks. Maybe that's nonsense, or maybe, like aeroplanes, magic evolves with time."

"You think witches used to fly on broomsticks?" she asked him skeptically, and he laughed.

"That goes back a long way and involves henbane and applications on areas of the body that it's not appropriate for me to discuss with you outside of a classroom. But witches, with their abilities to do harm or good, have been around for hundreds of years. Maybe we just have a media warped way of looking at them."

She blew her breath out on a huff and rubbed her hands over her eyes again. Jonas touched her, and she saw things in her head. She'd seen Nate with blue flames on his palms. Her headache left her as abruptly as it came after Matt touched her. She'd seen his nose bleeding, apparently from taking the pain from her. She'd seen the waterwheel when she'd fitted on Monday. Then they'd taken her to their favourite place, with a waterwheel exactly as she'd seen. It brought on a vivid, chilling hallucination. But what if it wasn't a hallucination? What if they were telling her the truth, and she was seeing things? What if it hadn't been a cruel joke? If they really were what they said they were? That Nate really was holding flames, that they were fairies?

Just the thought of it made her catch her breath. It was too much, too fantastical.

"Lily, I learnt a long time ago to have an open mind. I may not be able to understand why something is, but that doesn't mean it isn't. It's pretty arrogant to insist something isn't real just because we have no understanding of it, or it doesn't fit our preconceived way of thinking."

His words struck a chord deep inside her. Was she being arrogant? Or was she being realistic? She was so sure that they were playing a trick on her, but what if she was wrong? They'd only looked after her today. The twins gave her one of their wetsuits. They'd stopped those boys from throwing her around in the quarry. Matt helped her back to shore. They'd looked after her at college. There was no indication that they were playing a prank on her. If they'd been laughing at her, would they have gone to all that trouble? Plus, Jonas was a teacher; someone who could usually be trusted. Would he have willingly played a part in a trick that cruel? And on someone he didn't even know? It was highly unlikely.

She remembered Nate's suspicion. He'd been cautious of her at first, and maybe with good reason if what they'd said was right. If they really were Fae, they would have to be careful of anyone they met. Maybe that was why they hadn't made closer friends with anyone else. It started to make sense in her head, and with it the realisation that maybe, just maybe, she'd been wrong.

Drew shifted in his seat to turn towards her, and the sudden movement cut through her thoughts. "So, to answer your question: Do I believe in magic? Yes, I do believe in magic." He smiled softly at her. "But I have a feeling the real question here is, do you believe in magic, Lily?"

"I didn't," she admitted, staring at the knot in his tie. "But maybe I was wrong."

"Ah! Being wrong," he whispered. "Happens to the best of us. So, is that what you were arguing about?" he asked her quietly. "Or was this just academic?"

With a start she realised just how odd her questions must have seemed to him. "Academic," she said hastily. She caught his eyes, and he smiled at her. His eyes weren't soulless, how strange that she had thought they were. They were dark, almost black, but they sparkled with humour, intelligence, and something else; something she couldn't quite put her finger on.

"Well, in that case, you came to the right person," he said, switching off the engine. "I'm researching smuggling at the moment, but I love all British history. I have papers and books on the witch trials in Britain, especially the Pendle witches. You are more than welcome to read them."

"You've researched witches then?" she asked. He smiled at her, his head dropped slightly and for a fleeting second he looked evil. A ripple of unease made her breathing quicken, her hand released her belt, and she reached for the door handle.

"It seems ironic, considering your question was out of the blue," he said quietly, making her hesitate. "But, yes, I have. It's fascinating reading. You are more than welcome to read anything I have. A lot of my books are back home in Wick, but you are more than welcome to come in and see the ones I brought with me."

He was smiling at her again, his face perfectly calm, open and friendly. She was beginning to think she really had lost her mind. There was nothing evil about him. He was just her neighbour, a history professor, a teacher for goodness sake, he was perfectly safe. He'd sparked an interest in her now. She debated going in with him to have a look. It wouldn't hurt. A few minutes would be fine.

A car horn startled her, and realisation slammed into her that she shouldn't really go into his house without someone knowing where she was. She took her belt off and scrambled out of the car. She turned and looked back in at him. He was smiling at her as if she amused him. "Thank you for the lift back, but I really should get home." She was a little breathless, and it made him chuckle.

"A rain check?" he asked, and she found herself smiling back at him.

"Yes, a rain check," she said and shut the door. She ran around the back of his car and in through her gate. She didn't look back; she didn't acknowledge him again, wondering why on earth she'd agreed to a rain check with him. She heard his car drive around the corner of the last cottage where the car parking area was. She heard another car drive past, and she realised they'd been blocking the road. She reached her door and groaned aloud, she didn't have her bag and her mother still wasn't home.

She let her forehead rest against the door in exhausted defeat. She had a lot to think about, but the frightening part was the thought that maybe they were telling her the truth.

"Here."

She jumped, letting out a squeal and spinning on the spot to see Nate standing behind her. He held her bag in one hand and the wetsuit in the other. She bit her lip, unable to look into his eyes. It sank in that they must have left Jonas's place just after she had. They'd brought her things, knowing she had no way of getting in. They were looking after her again, even though she'd yelled and run out on them. She was completely turned about, overwhelmed and scared.

"I can't..." she faded out, taking them from him without looking up. She dug her key out of the side pocket, still unable to look at him.

"I know," he said quietly. "We'll still be here when you're ready, Lily May. We'll always be here for you." He turned and walked away.

"Nate!" His name left her lips before she thought about it. He turned to look at her, but she didn't know what else to say. She saw Matt and the twins coming up the road towards the gate, worry and concern filled their faces. She cracked, sagging slightly. She couldn't leave it like this. She needed to know one way or the other.

"Do you... do you want a coffee?" It was lame, and she knew it was, but she saw the raw relief on their faces and it settled her slightly. She unlocked the door and looked back over her shoulder at them, but her eyes fell on Drew. He was by his own door, his face cast in shadow from the porch. He raised his hand in a wave and went in, shutting the door behind him. She still had his handkerchief. She'd have to wash it and return it to him, she thought vaguely as she went inside. She heard the living room door shut, and she drew in a deep breath, turning to face them. There really was only one thing she could do now.

"Show me again," she whispered, bracing herself for an action that was going to change the rest of her life.

Nate lifted his palm, a small blue ball of flames flickered about two inches above his skin.

"Touch the flame, Lily May," he murmured. "I promise, it will not hurt you. We will never hurt you. Not intentionally."

She lifted shaky fingers and took a leap of faith, or doubt, she wasn't sure which. Her fingertips could feel the warmth from the fire, but it stayed a mild warmth as her fingers dipped through the blue flames. She wiggled her fingers, awe filling her. She blew onto the flames, but they didn't even waver. He lowered his palm, but the blue flames stayed in place. He lifted his other hand and snapped his fingers, the blue ball disappeared immediately.

"Oh, god," she muttered, her legs giving out on her as the blood drained from her head. Josh caught her in his arms and lowered her to sit on the floor with him. The others crouched around her, but they made no move to touch her.

"We have a lot to talk about, Lily Flower," Matt murmured.

"My life will never be the same, will it?" she whispered, aware of Josh's arms around her. She had to believe, even though she still didn't understand any of it. She had to believe that magic was real, that they were fairies.

"No," Nate said gently. "Things are going to change for you, Lily May, but you're not alone."

Tears slid down her face, and he reached out and caught one on his fingertip. He blinked and then held it out to her; a small blue crystal lay where her tear had been. Her heart missed a beat; that was no parlour trick.

"Lily, we want to help you understand what we are, what you are," Matt said quietly. She blew out her breath, taking the tiny crystal in her fingers. It was as tangible as she was. There was no denying this.

"Let us help you," Josh whispered.

"We won't hurt you, ever," Jake added.

Some things seem impossible because we don't understand it, but it doesn't stop it from being true or real.

Drew's words echoed in her head, and she nodded. She couldn't deny it any longer. She wanted to understand exactly what they were.

"Okay," she whispered. Their collective sigh of relief was almost covered by the shuffling noise as they surrounded her, pulling her into them, holding her tightly between them.

"You're one of us, Lily May. We'll always be here for you."

The words echoed through her head. She didn't know fully what they were, or what they could do. They were mistaken about her, though. She did know that much; there was nothing special about her. She didn't know what tomorrow would bring, or what would happen next. But their words wrapped around her, settling her deep inside; a sense of peace and belonging filled her.

She was where she belonged: with them. With them she'd finally found home.

No matter what they were.

Drew

Drew snarled as he shut the door. They were a complication he hadn't anticipated. He hadn't expected four hormonal teenage boys to be sniffing around her like bloodhounds. She was his, and he wasn't about to let nearly eighteen years of patiently waiting go to waste because of a bunch of schoolboys.

He'd seen them drive towards the car just as Lily got in. He'd driven off quickly, not wanting to give them the chance to talk her out of his car. He'd been tempted to drive away with her then. Tell her everything and take her away with him. But they'd tailed him, and in this day and age kidnapping was not as easy as it had once been. With mobile phones, satellite tracking, and the internet, the world was too small a place to use methods that once would have worked. No, he'd have to win her trust, and with them hovering around her like bees around a honey pot, it wasn't going to be easy.

He'd been watching her for years, waiting, making himself known enough times to frighten Lynda into moving on. He'd stopped Lily from putting down roots, from forming friendships that could interfere with his plans for her. He'd known about the visits to the doctors who had labelled it cryptogenic epilepsy because they couldn't find a reason for the apparent seizures. He'd watched as Lynda tried different medications in a vain attempt to block Lily's ability. Nothing the medical profession gave her worked, and in desperation she'd turned to the exact source she was trying to hide Lily from. Magic.

The pills Lynda gave her were effective to a point, but they were like plugging a hole in a bucket with cotton wool and then trying to fill it with water. They could only contain so much. And just as the water would eventually drip through, Lily's abilities had spilled out, all hidden under the lie of epilepsy. Lynda had denied her the right to her heritage. It made him furious to think about it, but at the same time it played into his hand. Lily would be much easier to control when she found out her whole life was built upon a lie. That the one person she thought she could trust had lied about everything to her. Every foundation that woman built for Lily was about to be demolished, and he would make damn sure he was there to pick up the pieces that would be left.

It was ironic, really, how Lynda's lies had aided his plans. Being epileptic was another reason why Lily was different from everyone around her, another reason why she found it difficult to fit in anywhere. And she never did fit in anywhere, never had close friends. Except for now. Now it seemed as if she'd caught the attentions of those boys. He would have to find another way to get close to her now that it wasn't just her and Lynda as he had expected.

He'd seen her in town twice, the first time he'd watched her go into the optician's. He'd deliberately placed himself so she would have to talk to him. Having her run headlong into him had been a stroke of luck he'd immediately seized upon. But the two boys she'd been with reacted instantly; he'd seen the animosity rolling off them as they'd taken a position behind her, warning him away from her. It was a clearly possessive manoeuvre, and one that told him that, on their part at least, she was theirs. He'd completely ignored them, not even acknowledging their presence. He wasn't going to get into it with two snotty nosed kids in front of her. The more harmless she thought he was, the better it would be for them both.

It was pure chance that he saw her running down the road, clearly upset. He'd been on business in the town and was returning to his cottage when he'd spotted her. It was hell sent and he took the opportunity, using it to his advantage.

Lily was oblivious that the boys had followed them all the way to Trenance, but he'd seen the anger on their faces when she'd got into his car. He'd debated letting them see him reach out and touch her shoulder when they stopped behind the tractor, but he wouldn't put it past them to ram their car into his, and he did like this car.

Although he wasn't completely certain that they were just schoolkids. Her question had thrown him for a second. It was a question that was a hundred miles from what he expected her to say. He guessed it was somehow linked to arguing with the boys, which led him to suspect that they'd said something to her, or she'd seen something around them that she'd found hard to believe. And judging by her headlong flight down the road, with tears pouring down her face, he figured it frightened her as well. It meant he would have to do some digging around to find out more about them. But until he knew what he was dealing with, his best defence was ignoring them.

He wasn't here for them, he was here for Lily. It was Lily he had to win over. Except he wasn't certain that he was winning her over. At one point she relaxed completely with him, but when those idiot boys honked the Land Rover horn, he'd seen fear in her eyes; and he'd realised that he was the one that had frightened her. He'd moved too quickly, asking her to go in with him. And he could kick himself for telling her he lived in Wick. But either she didn't know exactly where in Glastonbury she was born, or she didn't know Wick was in Glastonbury. Whatever the reason, she hadn't made the connection, and he'd sighed in relief. He would have to build her trust slowly and carefully, without revealing anything about who he was. He wasn't going to let anything, or anyone, ruin this for him. He'd waited too long and sacrificed too much for her.

He'd messed up with her mother, he wouldn't mess up with her.

The Seer Series
In order of reading:

Lily
Denial
Deceptive Secrets

Available at:
www.books2read.com/lily
www.books2read.com/denial
www.books2read.com/deceptivesecrets

Book 4 coming soon.

Acknowledgments

Thank you for reading this is book.

If you enjoyed it, please consider leaving a review on Goodreads and on the site where you purchased it.

Thank you for supporting independent authors.

I would like to thank Jennifer Leigh Jones and Rebecca Stewart for their hard work, unfailing support, and immense patience for putting up with me. I would still be floundering in a sea of confusion without them.

There are a lot of people I also want to thank, and a lot of you know who you are. Overseas and closer to home. Special thanks to the Ministry of Mayhem for unstinting support. Ripley Proserpina for not telling me where to go when I text at ungodly hours, due to being on the opposite side of the pond, and for responding with grace.

I couldn't have done this without all of you and countless others.

Much love.

Printed in Great
Britain
by Amazon